THREADS of COURAGE

THREADS of COURAGE
A Quilting Story
Part 3

JODI BARROWS

© 2017
by Jodi Barrows

All rights reserved. No part of this book may be reproduced in any form without permission in writing from the publisher, except in the case of brief quotations embodied in critical articles or reviews.

Edited by Linda Stubblefield, Affordable Christian Editing
Interior design: scottcornelius.net
Author photo: Holly Paulson Photography
Cover design & photography: scottcornelius.net
Printer: Color House Graphics, Grand Rapids, Michigan

Barrows, Jodi.
　Threads of courage: a quilting story. Part 3 / Jodi Barrows.

ISBN: 978-0-9994154-0-5

This is a work of fiction. Names, characters, places, and incidents either are the product of the author's imagination or are used fictitiously, and any resemblance to actual persons, living or dead, businesses, companies, events, or locales is entirely coincidental.

Printed in the United States of America

www.squareinasquare.com

FEBRUARY 1860

FORT WORTH, TEXAS

Chapter 1

Emma secured her brown, curly locks in a cloth scarf and tied her white apron firmly behind her back. She lifted a large iron pot of splashing water onto the stove and stoked the fire.

"One thing I can't get used to and still don't like is making soap and washing clothes," Emma said more to herself than to anyone.

She checked the temperature of the water on the stove one more time and gathered her soap-making supplies. The lye soap, borax, and ammonia were already on the kitchen table. Next she hauled the heavy lard bucket across the wood floor, making a scraping sound with each tug.

I never knew while growing up at the Mississippi plantation that making soap was such hot, hard work. Nellie and the house slaves did all the laundry. If I ever see her again, I will hug her neck and tell her thank you. How she missed Nellie, her black maid, and often wondered how she was doing. They had parted with tears in their eyes, vowing to find each other again.

She seldom thought about Mississippi or her father's heavy-handedness with her family. *I still don't understand why my father wouldn't let Nellie come with me when I came west. It must just have been meanness on his part.* Emma could come up with no other answer.

The years since Emma and her sister Abby had left with their Mailly cousins had flown by, and she knew she was the better for leaving. She had finally found her way and had discovered who she was meant to be. She was happier and more content than she ever thought she could be. No one in Texas told her she couldn't do it. In fact, they encouraged her to think, be independent and get after her dreams. She certainly didn't take long in finding out what "it" was. But she knew the soap chore of today wasn't "it" and was even now ready to be done with it!

Emma heaved the bucket up on the table and wiped her brow with the corner of her apron and sighed. "I sure do miss her."

Emma's cousin, Megan, covered her smile as she watched the young woman struggle with her work. Megan had seen Emma grow in her confidence since she had left her father's oppressive home. The green-eyed beauty was once quiet and sulky, but now full of worth and purpose. Emma had blossomed in the freedom that Texas offered the women who were willing to leave friends, family and the security of home. Women, who were regarded as equals in this new frontier, were expected to pull their share of the load.

"I'm sorry, I wish I could help you more," Megan said as she sat at the table with a very round belly showing under her apron. "We consistently made the soap and did the laundry and never knew any different. Liz always made it part of the chore list. I can measure the ingredients without looking at Granny's recipe," she commented, now standing and measuring them for Emma.

"I can remember the one can of lye, one quart of hot water and two quarts of lard, but I've forgotten the other things—probably 'cause I want to!" Emma chuckled. She mixed the three ingredients together and waited for them to come to a boil.

"We usually made the soap outside because it boiled over so much. I like doing it inside when it is cold and rainy out, like today," Megan added, pushing aside a shiny, light-brown lock of hair.

Emma had combined the final ingredients—one tablespoon of borax, one cup of ammonia and a half cup of warm water in a bowl—while waiting for the first mixture to boil and cool again. Megan placed cool glasses of water on the table for her and her cousin and then took her seat again.

"How often do you feel the baby?" Emma asked, looking at the uncomfortable Megan.

Megan swallowed her sip of water and ran her hand over her expanding midsection with a loving touch. "Almost constantly. Very active little thing. Since this is my first, I don't quite know what to expect. Liz said all three of her babies were different." Megan quickly thought back to her sister's accounts of her experiences.

Emma listened and couldn't imagine a separate life growing inside her body. She had been at most of the deliveries during the baby boom in Fort Worth and was still in awe over the whole birthing process. Liz, Megan's older sister, had married Thomas only a few weeks after their arrival in Fort Worth and had Mattie within the first year, then Sofie just a stair step behind her sister. Megan had married Jackson between Liz's girls coming along and was now due with her first. Her sister Abby, the schoolteacher, would be soon married, and the way things were going, would likely have her first baby before school was out the next spring.

Emma felt sure she could have been married to a number of gentlemen, ranchers or cowboys if she had let her wishes be known, but really her heart simply wasn't leading in that direction. She had just found her freedom from her father's restrictive life and was enjoying doing whatever she wanted. Most women had to marry to have a home and security, and how grateful she was not to be in that position! Maybe making soap and washing clothes were easier than she had thought after all. Other elements of a woman's life were certainly undesirable to her.

Megan stood to check both pots that had been brought to a boil.

While both were now cooling, the cousins had been somewhat lost in their own thoughts.

"Megan, stay away from those," Emma warned. "They are too hot, and your tummy is in the way." Both women chuckled, and Megan stepped back to let Emma check the soap.

"Well, at least, I can get the wooden boxes ready," she commented as she lined each box with a cotton cloth. Megan was used to doing her share of the work and found it hard to stand by idly.

"I'm going to make a few bars of soap with the lavender herbs. It smells so nice when we bathe with it." Emma poured both mixtures together to boil again and returned to the task at hand.

"When Liz goes back to the ranch, the soap will be set in the boxes and ready for her to use."

Emma admired her oldest cousin, Liz, who was the confident, firm leader in the family. She had a sweet disposition, cared for her family, worked hard, and possessed an ability to organize like none other. Emma had learned much from the blonde storekeeper, wife and mother. Liz carefully considered matters before making a suggestion, and then, everything seemed to fall into place.

In the beginning, Emma had wondered if Liz were simply a female likeness of her father, but she soon learned that Liz was guided by love and only wanted to encourage Emma, not control her. Somehow, Liz was always a step ahead of her family, ready with what was needed at exactly the right time. As Emma watched her older cousin operate in love, she wished her own temper wasn't quite as quick as it was. She was working on being more patient and keeping her mouth shut just a little more often. But sometimes the words simply tumbled out before she even thought them through.

Liz and Megan shared the responsibilities at the Mercantile they owned. Liz had two little girls and divided her time between the ranch and the general store. Megan helped out on the days Liz stayed at the ranch. *The arrangement has been working well,* Megan thought. *But with my own little one due most any time, things are sure to become a handful.* The baby inside of her kicked as if agreeing with her thoughts.

"Guess I'm not much help with the soap making," Megan sighed and adjusted her position, making room for the wriggling body she carried. "I think this baby is propping his feet on my ribs and pushing."

Emma laughed and looked at the movement of Megan's tummy. "That's okay; you have always been there to help me. Remember when the first herd of cattle came through town and the cooking mess I got into? You and Luke sure helped me out of that one!" Thinking back made her realize how much she missed that young man. She thought of Luke as a younger brother, not a distant cousin. Luke was Liz's firstborn with her husband, Caleb, when they lived at the Mailly timber mill in Louisiana. Now a young man with Caleb's same good looks, Luke worked at his stepfather Thomas' ranch, just a half-day's ride from town.

Megan held her stomach as she laughed. "Don't forget about renting out the bathhouse too! That was another time we boiled water all day."

Emma was about to pour the bubbling brew into the boxes so they would harden into bars. Megan stood ready with the crushed lavender.

"When will Jackson be back in town?" Emma asked about Megan's husband, who served as both a Ranger and a rancher.

"I'm not sure...with more Comanche problems west and north of us." Megan paused. "But the U.S. military believes they can handle the situation without the help of the Rangers." She shook her head. "And I ask you, are they here? What would we do if we needed help?"

Megan vigorously stirred several spoonfuls of crushed lavender into the thick soap mixture. "Right now, I think he is at the ranch with Thomas unless trouble has transpired somewhere."

Emma tried not to express her worries over Megan's husband and his responsibilities. "Do you think he would accept the sheriff's job here in Fort Worth? The town has grown so much over the past years since we first arrived. Cattle drives occasionally come our way, and a number of the cowboys are nothing more than outlaws in disguise. My little restaurant can hardly keep up on weekends."

Emma had opened a small restaurant shortly after she and her sister had settled in Fort Worth. Seemingly, they were feeding everyone in the expanding Texas territory. The scent of the fresh, homemade meals that waltzed out her doors drew everyone her way, whether or not they were hungry. Eventually, the town's residents and visitors alike all found their way to her table.

Whether or not she meant to name her restaurant, "Emma's Table," the designation became a natural fit. Her friend, Chet, another cowboy at the ranch and a good friend of the Mailly family had burned the name onto a smooth oak board and then had placed it over the door for her as a surprise. The reserved, young woman liked the way naming her place had made her feel. The sense of worth, hard work and responsibility was a feeling that hadn't come along much in her short life. Liz and Megan trusted her and encouraged her to follow through with her ideas. The resulting sparkle in her green eyes was quite becoming.

She cooked for the locals who came into town on the weekends for their supplies from her cousin's general store or maybe for a group of drovers who had settled their herd on the outskirts of town. Drifters as well as pioneers heading west in wagon trains all enjoyed the mouth-watering fare of "Emma's Table."

Emma had discovered she enjoyed cooking and had honed her skills cooking for the family. She soon learned to cook extra for whoever stumbled along. The unexpectedness of operating a restaurant was enjoyable to her. Her life had been so humdrum before she had left to go west with her cousins a few years ago. Now excitement and adventure filled her daily life.

She usually had a variety of foods to offer and always had a round of meals continually cooking. A pot of brown beans bubbled on her stove everyday as well as cornbread and her famous mouth-watering biscuits fresh from the oven. They were the flakiest anyone had ever tasted and had become her signature dish. She used the same biscuit mix to make her peach cobbler almost year round. Even if a person was as full as a tick, he managed to make room for a bowl of the sweetness. In the summer, she would even can jars of peaches in order to serve cobbler year round. When the blackberries were ripe, she would prepare the blackberry cobbler that Chet, the cowboy at Liz and Thomas' ranch, loved most of all. She would save some back for him—in case he would show up unexpectedly. He was always good for a laugh and willing to help her with any chore that didn't come easy to her.

Both women worked silently, lost in their own thoughts as they finished the batch of soap. Emma finally set the empty kettle down and looked at the bars of soap. Several wooden boxes held the scented soap, and others held the laundry soap. Success! Though Megan and Emma were more scattered with responsibilities these days, they continued to share the workload as much as possible. Today had been no different.

"Are we going to make another batch for the Mercantile? Liz sells it pretty well. I heard some of the cowboys even keep a bar in their saddle bags." Emma wiped her brow again and looked at her with evident compassion. "You okay?" She noticed Megan seemed quite pale.

Megan twisted in her chair. "I think so. I'm just so uncomfortable, and now I'm all stirred up over the news about the cavalry and the sheriff job. I get lost in the worry of my thoughts, and it doesn't help one bit!"

"I'm sorry I got you thinking on it," Emma apologized.

"It doesn't matter," Megan sighed. "Seems the thoughts are always lingering there."

Emma wondered if marriage and having the children that came with a husband was what she really wanted. *I can certainly get one of the many little ones in my family to play with if I have a hankering for a baby! Then I can just return the wee one to his mother when I'm tuckered out.*

Liz's youngest little girl, Sofie, toddled out of the bedroom, rubbing her eyes after a long nap. She tried to curl up in Megan's nonexisting lap.

"Hey, sweetheart, how was your nap?" Megan molded the little cherub around her tummy and smoothed the blonde curls from her face. Still sleepy, she rested her head on her aunt's shoulder and giggled.

"Baby!" she smiled and looked at Megan.

Megan smiled back and asked, "Can you feel the baby wiggle?"

Emma smiled too as she started another batch of soap to sell at the Mercantile.

Sofie started to put her thumb in her mouth but didn't when Megan shook her head. "Sofie's a big girl." Megan encouraged the little one with her right decision.

"I'm really not happy with Jackson being a Ranger, a sheriff or a federal marshal," she suddenly declared. "Seems to me that a gun and some stupid cowboy, outlaw, or Indian is going to cause me heartache someday."

Emma stirred the soap as Megan expressed her heart. She felt the same way but couldn't let Megan know.

"Well," Megan added, "we can't worry about it. We just have to trust the good Lord to take care of Jackson." Megan knew that's what Liz would say, so she went ahead and said it. She seemed to be having thoughts on exactly who the good Lord was. She had worked out a lot of her thoughts and personal problems since coming West and being allowed to be herself and not a molded Southern society woman. But the issue of God and who He really was and what He wanted baffled her. Taking the belief because her family did wasn't good enough. She knew God had to become real to her. She didn't hear Him like Liz did.

Sofie mumbled around her fist, "Mama?"

"Yes, sweetheart, I will take you over to your mother at the Mercantile, but first we need to get your shoes and wash your face and comb your pretty curls. We can get a cookie from Emma's cookie jar if you stop at the outhouse on the way."

Sofie's curls bounced as she looked for the cookie jar. Emma already had the lid half off and was wrapping a cookie in a cloth. After Sofie had slid off her aunt's lap, Megan put the cookie in her apron pocket when she stood up. Emma smiled at the sight of the two of them waddling out the door, chattering away.

Chapter 2

The first spring the Maillys were in Texas, they had planted an orchard only a stone's throw from the Captain's house. Grapevines had been placed along one fence line on one side of the rows of peach and pecan trees. Along the other side of the orchard were blackberry bushes and then the thicket of the woods. The family was already enjoying a bounty of produce from their plantings.

Situated between the house and the orchard were Emma's hen houses. Her chicken business had turned into a full-time job, and she took great pride in her work. She had conceived the idea on her own and brought it to life with her own thoughts and actions. Raising chickens wasn't her Texas dream, but she enjoyed her responsibility and the independence the thriving business gave her. This sense of accomplishment would have never happened on her father's plantation.

Liz had brought chickens from Louisiana when they had moved to Fort Worth and now had several varieties of her own. She had helped Emma pick out the chickens she wanted to raise. She enjoyed the Rhode Island Reds, which were certainly pretty as far as chickens go. Emma loved the chicken's tall red feathers, and the good money she earned on this breed. Another variety she enjoyed was the Buff Orpingtons, her "Buffs," as she called them. Their feathers were like rainbows with a metallic shine to them. The newest breed of chickens in her house were Bantam chickens. These miniature chickens with their big personalities, which were also called Bantys, were about half the size of her other hens.

Threads of Courage

Fort Worth's weather had been cold and rainy, so Emma kept a sharp eye on her chickens. If they became too wet, they could get the droop and die. She certainly didn't want to lose any of her flock, so she waited patiently for the sprinkles to stop. The time had also come to encourage the brooding hens to begin setting on their next batch of eggs so she would have a spring hatch of chicks.

The back door of her restaurant opened, and Emma appeared in her hooded cape. She then walked out to the hen houses to check on the condition of her hens. As she inspected each pen, she double-checked the latches on the doors. Before the rains had come, she had noticed a grey fox living in the orchard that had become a little too brave about approaching her hen houses. With her latest bunch of chicks only a fence away from danger, no chances could be taken.

Right as Emma turned to take one last look, she saw the tail of a serpent twist under the wall of her nesting hens. Frantic, she looked for the hoe or the shovel that always rested nearby. *They're gone!* Emma knew that someone's or something's life could be hanging on that shovel not being returned to its proper place.

Emma pulled a loose board from the chicken house wall and entered the darkness of the coop. Just as her eyes adjusted, she saw the chicken snake had slithered up to the second shelf and now had an egg in its mouth. Emma started to beat the trespasser with the board as it turned and glided toward its access hole.

Emma struck the snake again and again, screaming with each resounding thud. The chickens were squawking and flying about, their feathers floating everywhere. One bird had even managed to entangle itself in her cape and flapped about, further upsetting Emma. Realizing it couldn't escape through the opening with the egg in its mouth, the snake finally dropped its meal to retreat hastily. By the time Emma had removed the bird from her hood, rescued the undamaged egg and returned it to the proper nest, the snake had retreated into the safety of the thicket behind the coop.

Muttering to herself, Emma came out through the gate of the fenced pen, looking as though she had been in a fierce battle. Her curls had fallen down around her face, and her cape was twisted about her shoulders. The board was still in her bruised hands as she marched fiercely toward the back door of her restaurant.

At the back door of the nearby Mercantile, Liz stood with her shotgun in hand and her two little girls peeking from behind her skirt. Mattie, her oldest, started to run down the stairs to see about her Emma. "Em!" she shouted as she ran to her favorite family member.

Two cowboys, who had been eating at the restaurant, came running from the back door. They had grown concerned after hearing all of the screaming and commotion. As they came closer, they started to chuckle when they saw Emma with feathers caught in her hair and cape. "Ma'am, you all right?" the concerned duo asked in between snickers.

Mattie giggled too. "Em, you have feathers for hair."

"I must look as frantic as I feel," Emma said, watching the feathers float around her as she tried to shake them off. "I can't believe I let a chicken snake get away! All I could find to fight with was this loose board I pulled from the coop." Exasperated, she tossed it at the gate where it struck with a heavy thud.

"Miss Emma, you need a hoe close to your coops," one of the cowboys hesitantly offered, as if the idea had never been considered before.

"Yes, I do," Emma stated flatly. "Thank you. I've been watching for a fox, and I wasn't expecting a snake in the rain. I can usually smell a snake, but I can't smell a snake when it's been raining. I guess I let my guard down—about scared the life out of me!" She looked back at the hen house and continued to remove the feathers from her garments. "You boys get back to your meal," she said as she slowly calmed down. "Thank you, but I'm fine. I'll be back in to get your peach cobbler in just a minute or two."

Emma stood and watched a few more feathers float by. Liz chuckled as she came closer with her girls at her side and leaned the shotgun against the wall. She finished helping Emma remove the loose feathers as she picked up the still-frightened Sofie.

Sofie settled on her mother's hip and promptly popped her thumb into her mouth. Her big eyes stared at her rumpled aunt as she started to whimper.

Liz pulled out Sofie's thumb as she said, "No, Sofie. Emma's okay; you don't need to be afraid. A big snake was trying to get her baby chicks."

Sofie looked toward the hen house, back to her momma and then at Emma as if to say she wasn't so sure.

Mattie, her eyes sparkling, asked with authority, "Did you get him?"

"No, but he won't be back. I beat him pretty bad, and he dropped the egg from his mouth without even cracking it!" Emma looked at her sore hands.

"Goody!" Mattie stated in her feisty, little-girl voice. "Mean ol' snake." With a scowl, the little girl turned and marched back into the Mercantile. Even though she wasn't in school yet, according to her, she ran her mother's general store.

"Emma, I'll make sure we have a new hoe put by the coop for you," Liz noted as she pulled the last feather from Emma's hood and straightened the shoulders of the cape. "Sure was quite a racket coming from that coop…" Liz giggled again and went inside with Sofie still looking toward the hen house over her mama's shoulder.

Chapter 3

Megan sat in a wooden rocker on the porch, enjoying the sun after so many cool, rainy days. She looked forward to the early spring Texas offered each year. Last spring she had married Jackson, the Ranger, and this year they would welcome their first baby. She rocked and smiled as she thought about her happiness. Her dream of a dress shop had never materialized, but the idea was of no concern to her. Maybe when the time was right she would venture forward with it. After all, Fort Worth was certainly growing.

Megan was busy enough helping Liz with two babies, the Mercantile and keeping the vexing, mischievous Emma out of hot water. She chuckled at the latest event involving the snake in the hen house. She enjoyed her work at the Mercantile as well as the customers who came in each day. She normally worked the first part of each week with Liz's working the last.

Liz and her daughters came into town from the ranch on Thursday and returned home after church on Sunday. They would stay above the Mercantile where she and Thomas had started their married life. Thomas worked at the ranch all week and then came into town Saturday afternoon, like the rest of the ranch hands. After church and a big family dinner on Sunday, the entire family would return to the Rolling M.

Megan wasn't sure how her baby would affect the schedule. Her life wasn't very normal anyway. Jackson had often been in Fort Worth until they married, and now he seemed to be gone more than he was home. She and Jackson took her room at the Mailly house where Abby and Emma still shared a room. The Mailly house continued to be a meeting place for the family. Megan's baby kicked, so she patted her tummy to calm the little one.

The baby boom in the community had worn out much of the passed-around items that the women shared. Anna Parker's Hope Rose had used them, and before her, Iris—Katie Longmont's fourth baby. Next in line to share had been Mattie and Sofie, Liz's two little girls. When the box had been passed to Megan, she took one look and immediately ordered fabric from the Mercantile. Her sewing skills came to good use as she cut and sewed new garments and quilts for her the one to arrive soon. She even made a few new items for her nieces.

She was also busy sewing Abby's wedding dress as her cousin, the schoolteacher, would be marrying Samuel, the town's lawyer, in a few weeks. After a couple of years of persistent attention from the city official, she had given in and said yes. They would tie the knot in the spring when her students took time off from school to work in the fields. Her final decision to marry happened when Samuel promised he would build her a house soon after they wed. Meanwhile, Abby would move to Samuel's home above the law office on Main Street. Megan, known as the matchmaker, was pleased about this marriage and happy for them both. She still didn't understand why it took Abby so long to decide to marry Samuel.

So much had changed since the Mailly girls had bumped into the town of Fort Worth with their eight wagons. Texas had promised them a new start. The growth of Fort Worth had boomed with the availability of cheap land, plenty of timber and an abundant water supply. The growing season was two thirds of the year with mild temperatures and consistent rains.

Many settlers were planting their homes in Tarrant and Parker County, preferring the quiet, rural lifestyle to rear and educate their families. Because of this rapid growth, Fort Worth continued to hold the county records, and a special election had been planned for the spring. Even plans to build a stone courthouse were in the works, making Fort Worth the permanent county seat. The main street boasted several new storefronts and a flour mill. Cattle drives and wagon trains added to the commotion, which resulted in a regular flow of money through town.

The coming war didn't hurt the growth of Texas. Mississippi and many other Confederate states sold out, moving lock, stock and barrel to the frontier. They had written "Gone to Texas" in large letters across their front doors and never thought about it again. The state's population had increased almost two hundred percent with most of the newcomers living on the frontier. What a contrast to the elegant, civilized cities along the Mississippi River! The threats of the West were of less concern than the ominous images of war, and Southern families had been relocating along the roughest of landscapes. Liz and Megan saw new faces in the Mercantile almost weekly, and their sales were booming.

❋ ❋ ❋

Jackson had been riding with the 2nd Cavalry as they teamed up with the Tonkawa scouts for the Antelope Hill expedition. After the battle of Little Robe Creek and the roundup to send all of the Indian tribes to a reserved area of land on the prairies north of them, Texas had penetrated the heart of the Comanche forces, or so they hoped. But with these attacks exhausting the government's budget, funds had been withdrawn, and the Rangers were ordered to disband.

That's when Megan's frustrated new husband was hired on at Thomas' ranch, only to be in town on weekends. If he accepted the job of federal marshal, he would be in town more often, but still not permanently. She wasn't satisfied with any of the job prospects as each one required him to carry a gun and to be away from home on a regular basis.

Colt, the other Ranger, who rode with Jackson and Tex, accepted a sheriff's position not far away in the community of Birdville. Tex stayed on at being a Ranger even though no money was available to pay him. He was just too old and too stubborn to change. Most of the time, he chose to stay in the Fort Worth area, ring the school bell and hone his reading skills with Abby, the schoolmarm.

Maybe their grandfather had been right after all, as they could all feel the unrest of a war only a beat away. Grandfather had always believed the country was heading for a war, which was the very reason they had sold out and moved in the first place. Texas was torn between seceding and whether or not to be a slave state. Most of the slaves were held in East Texas with North Texas holding mostly free, skilled labor of black men and women. The governor, who had worked so hard at joining the Union, was brokenhearted over the Democrats' talk in Austin of joining the Confederacy if the predicted war did break out.

Once again, the state wanted the right to choose and not to be told how to vote concerning slavery. The presidential election was heating up in the papers. A man named Lincoln was often in the headlines for his anti-slavery views, even though his wife's family, the Todds, owned slaves. Sam Houston, the new governor of Texas, did not want to see his great state throw that away by seceding with the other Southern states.

Texas had been the first state to build settlements west of the Mississippi or the Missouri Rivers. The fiercely independent and proud men who came to Texas weren't afraid of hardship, and none had a lazy bone or any thought of drunkenness in them. They were Texans first and Americans second. Texas had been fought over, pushed, pulled and prodded by Mexico, Spain, France and the United States. It was just natural for a Texan to fight for freedom; fight was in his blood. The promise of fat cattle, sizable forests, abundant game, rich soil, fresh water, and room to grow motivated twenty thousand settlers to pour into Texas in less than three years. They planted cotton and sugar cane and raised cattle. These hardy settlers fought off outlaws, Indians and criminals. Wicked weather or wild animals didn't discourage them. No one could tell them what to do.

When the United States government sent Sam Houston to govern the fledgling state, Houston appealed to the independent Texasians for competent, fighting men to build a standing army. His call to arms was answered by men like Davy Crockett, Jim Bowie, and Colonel William B. Travis, who gave their lives at the Alamo in Texas' birthing pains.

❀ ❀ ❀

Megan's heart started beating faster, and her head was swimming with the unknown as she thought about all of the disorder. She worried that right as she and the other women married and began having children, their men would be called away to fight.

Dropping her sewing in a basket, she stood to pace the porch. Wearily, she rubbed her forehead. *I must calm down from this ridiculous worry.* She grabbed the railing as her vision began to fade, and the porch began to spin.

Chapter 4

Abby watched over her students as they sat writing on real paper tablets that had come all the way from Mississippi. Her mother had tucked them in as a surprise with the wedding quilt she had sent for Abby and Samuel on the last stagecoach.

Since Fort Worth had been added to the stage line going West, a few packages and letters would be left at Liz's general store. Liz had added a U.S. Post Office to her business and would hold items until the neighboring folks came into town, mostly on weekends. Receiving the mail gave everyone a sense of excitement and even an adventure with not knowing what or when a parcel would show up.

On the day her wedding quilt arrived, Abby had gone to see Liz after settling an advanced primer in front of her two adult, after-school students, Mr. Graham and Ranger Tex. She hurried off, pushing through Liz's red doors of the Mercantile, almost upending Liz and knocking the parcel from her arms. She soon learned the package was for her from her mother in Mississippi. Unwrapping the package carefully, she smiled as she gazed at the stunning red and white quilt.

The quilt featured twelve identical, eighteen-inch white blocks with seventeen red triangle bursts on a half circle in each corner. The blocks were bordered on each side with nineteen red triangle points and sashed together with white rectangles. In each corner setting was a red-shaped circle. And, as if the quilt weren't already beautiful enough, red triangles ran down two sides of the border. Abby and Liz, both avid quilters, were speechless as they admired the gift.

Her parents were delighted with her upcoming marriage to Samuel Smith, a lawyer who owned land and served as a statesman. He was exactly what they had wanted for their daughter and were pleased she was ready to fit into their mold of a proper Southern woman. Abby had known exactly how to present her new husband to them in her letters home. Although she did feel a little deceitful for not revealing how very different life was in Texas. Compared with Mississippi, she and Samuel weren't anything like the upper society of Mississippi. She silently giggled to herself as she thought about a Texas barn dance with roasted, wild boar to eat compared to a Mississippi plantation society ball with slaves' serving a feast.

When she had first met Samuel, she thought of him as one of those arrogant Southern gentlemen and wanted nothing to do with him. She confirmed this assumption when she saw him with the politicians from Austin who came every year for the wolf hunt. They smoked cigars, drank bourbon and discussed the Union's pressing upon the Southern states, expressing views and opinions that didn't settle well with them.

She wanted nothing to do with the life he represented. She had seen the very life snuffed from her mother and her marriage dissolve into nothing but society rules and appearances. Abby would have none of it.

But Samuel was persistent, and over time, she saw he was not what she had assumed him to be. He was mannerly and educated, but he enjoyed life and expected the same for Abby. He didn't mind that she wanted to continue to teach school after they married and perhaps even continue when they had children. She understood he was a Texan first, then a lawyer and lastly a politician.

Threads of Courage

Yes, life was definitely different here in the West, and she loved her freedom. Samuel and the area in which she now lived had certainly taught her to relax. She wasn't the stuffy prim and proper schoolteacher of Mississippi anymore. Abby's class had never written with anything but slate and chalk and were now very quiet as their new pencils slid evenly over the tan paper. She marveled at how her class had changed over the past four years. When she had started teaching, she had every age in attendance from Katie Longmont's little boy who wasn't ready for learning to Luke and his friends who were bursting to get out of the classroom. Now those boys had steady employment at farms and ranches in the community. Little Dove, the Parkers' adopted Indian daughter, worked at Emma's restaurant, helping out with any task where she was needed. She was a sweet young lady and had become a real daughter to Anna and Pastor Heath Parker.

During this school year, Abby's classroom was filled with half-grown children who could read and write and work well on their own. Her teaching responsibilities had become relatively easy. The extra time had allowed her to plan her society wedding to Samuel, help Megan make a dress and further contemplate the path of her life more than she ever had before.

Quietly sliding back her chair, she stood and walked to the back of the classroom where she could feel the warmth of the sun shining through the window. How she loved to look out this window and admire the seasons as they came and went! The school was located where the countryside met the edge of Fort Worth. She found beauty even at the end of winter. With great anticipation, she watched spring approach around the corner as tiny buds on the trees waited impatiently for the sunshine to burst forth and declare the new season.

But the sight she most enjoyed at this window was the marvelous array of birds. Every day she saw chickadees with their white triangular masks over their dark heads and the round blue bodies of the titmouse proudly displaying the crests on top of their heads. In the spring and fall, the beautiful, velvet-looking cedar waxwings came foraging through the area, stopping to clear the berries off the cedar trees and taking splashy baths in any available puddle they could find.

Abby was silent in sweet reverence when a red cardinal appeared in the barren trees. The crimson male was easily seen as it fluttered about. Abby always saw the cardinals in pairs and sometimes as many as three sets of them. In the cold rain of winter, they remained silent, but when the sun came out, their song could be heard all morning long.

Her eyes drifted toward the hard-packed earth of the church cemetery where she quickly found the marker of Lucas Mailly. Blades of withered prairie grass gracefully waved in the silent breath of wind blowing across her grandfather's grave. With the passing of time, the grave was now flat and even with the earth around it. Abby wished he could have been here to see his family flourish. He had been wise about so many matters. *I still miss him. How I wish he could ring the bell for school every day, kiss Mattie and Sofie on the cheek, and walk me down the aisle when I marry Samuel.* A tear trickled down her cheek as she thought about her beloved grandfather. *He should be here with us.* Her eyes went to the fresh mound of dirt and wooden cross. She silently read the inscription: *"Smithy, best friend and blacksmith."* This was the place where her future father-in-law had been laid to rest.

For most of his life, Smithy had been a blacksmith for the Cavalry, moving his wife Rose and two children every time his men were required to go a little farther West. His wife had been buried several years before him, and now he rested next to her again. Their daughter Anna had married the army pastor, Heath Parker. Like Smithy, the couple had remained in Fort Worth in 1856, when the military was instructed to move farther West. Smithy stayed to become the town blacksmith and Parker the community preacher. Samuel, their son, had arrived in Fort Worth in 1854 after finishing law school and living in Austin for a spell. In 1856, Abby and her Mailly family came, opening the Mercantile and developing the freight line. Abby was hired to start the first school in the area.

So much had happened in the past four years—the deaths of friends and family and the birth of so many little girls. She had never thought of Samuel's father passing away. He was strong and seemed healthy enough, but one morning they found him in his bed, never to wake again. *The circle of life* she thought. *Grandfather's gone and now Smithy*. The only elderly man left in town was Tex, the Ranger, and she really didn't think of him in that way, but then she had not thought of her grandfather or Smithy as old. They were very able-bodied men.

"Teacher?" asked Sally, a new student, as she interrupted Abby's thoughts.

Abby quickly dabbed at the moisture on her cheek and turned to face her. Bending down to her level, she gently said, "Sally, remember? People will respect you when you respect them. It's important to use our manners. Please call me Miss Abby."

Sally was as timid as a church mouse, and Abby certainly didn't want to scare the sweet girl.

"Miss Abby, the clock chimed. It's time for us to go," Sally continued, obeying her teacher's request. "My mama needs me to hurry home today. I have a lot of chores."

Abby looked to the clock ticking on the wall. It was more than fifteen minutes past the time to release her students for the day.

"Oh, my, yes! All of you may go." She waved her hands toward the door to shoo her students on home. Hurrying to the entryway where their wraps and lunch pails were stored, the students quietly chatted as they slipped on their coats for the walk home. Soon they wouldn't even need to worry about the chill. Sally scarcely buttoned hers as she flew down the steps and ran toward the far edge of town. Sally's mother took in laundry and had plenty to do each day. Abby had even noticed clothes hanging on the line on Sundays. The little girl's father seemed to drink up most of their money. Most days he didn't even show up for work at the mill. Rumor had been tossed around that they had been kicked out of the wagon train that had passed through town last summer. She was glad Sally could attend her school.

Abby went to her desk to straighten her books and decided to leave early. She didn't need much planning for the next day. Megan had been sewing on her wedding gown, and she wanted to see the progress. Her cousin was quite talented and had designed it from a newspaper picture she had from back east. The row of buttons down the back was absolutely exquisite. Some of the women had laughed about all of the buttons, teasing her and saying she would have to start getting into her wedding dress the day before and sleep standing up! Megan had fussed about the back of her dress being the most important part with the bride's standing at the front of the church; her back would be most visible to the guests.

Megan had chosen silk that had to be shipped from Chicago and lace that had come from New York City. She had convinced Abby to crochet the button loops for the back of the dress—all seventy-two of them! The work of art also had a sweetheart neckline; long, lacy sleeves; and a full gathered skirt in the back with a princess waistline. Abby was certain to be the most beautiful bride in the state of Texas! She had worked hard to help Megan with the dress, sewing each evening with her cousin, but Megan was the true seamstress behind the gown. Wasting her talent here on the edge of civilization truly seemed a shame.

Although Liz and Emma had given up their corsets early on, Abby still wore hers every day. With her dress fitting so snugly, it was a good thing. Megan wasn't so sure she would continue to wear her corset after her baby came.

Samuel had many friends from the capital coming to Fort Worth, and Abby's dress would fit well into the society pages of Austin. As the growing city didn't yet have a suitable hotel, Samuel had been busy fixing up the army barracks for the extra guests coming to town. He had explained the accommodations to the guests, and they seemed excited for a quaint country visit. The details would fit perfectly into the story the newspaper in Austin was prepared to print. "Society Wedding on the Prairie" was already a headline. The men from Austin had been coming for the wolf hunt for years, and now their wives were joining them to observe the event for themselves. To experience the West and its ways was quite an adventuresome undertaking.

Abby's coat was draped over her arm as she walked the short distance home, enjoying the warm sun and hoping that spring was right around the corner. Consumed with her own thoughts, she walked up the steps onto the porch of the house she shared with Emma and Megan every day and Jackson on the weekends. Caught up in her reflections, she almost missed seeing the motionless body of her cousin, lying in a pool of blood.

Frantically, Abby yelled for help, hoping Liz or Emma would

hear her through the back doors of their stores. She tried to help Megan inside while continuing to yell. No one came.

She looked in Megan's sewing basket, sure she would find the pistol she knew her cousin kept there. Buried beneath some fabric scraps she found it, pointed it up and quickly fired two rounds, signaling for help. She saw the women rushing out of their back doors and running across the yard.

"Emma, run and get Anna or Samuel or Little Dove. Megan needs help. I…I think it's the baby."

Liz helped Abby get Megan into the house and out of her clothing. She tossed and mumbled as they laid her in bed.

"Jackson, Jackson…get Jackson," she murmured in despair.

"How do we get word to Jackson?" Abby asked as she worked, gathering soft rags to staunch the bleeding. "Oh, Liz, what are we to do? How do we stop this bleeding? The baby, oh, the sweet little one…"

"Pray, Abby. Pray hard. Anna will be here any time."

"We need a doctor—a real doctor," Abby insisted. "Fort Worth needs a doctor."

"Get some hot water, a basin and more towels. This baby is coming." Liz worked quickly and efficiently, not answering Abby.

Megan rolled with a new birthing pain and whimpered. Tears welled up in her eyes as her body shuddered with another contraction. Little Dove suddenly appeared in the doorway with Anna, and the two of them immediately started to help Liz with the care of Megan and her baby. Well into the evening, a pink, squalling little girl finally lay in the arms of a very weak, but alive, Megan.

"She's so tiny," Abby whispered, not sure the worst was over.

Anna washed her hands and looked pensively at the mother and baby. "I don't know how we saved the two of them. Megan couldn't have a drop of blood left in her. We will need a mother who is nursing to feed the baby while Megan regains her strength. She won't be able to feed the baby for a while, and we can't let her milk dry up before she has the strength to nurse the baby."

"I can," Liz offered. "Sofie still feeds at night, and I have milk. I will give this little girl my milk until Megan can."

"How do we get word to Jackson at the ranch?" Abby asked, still in quiet reverence over all that had transpired.

"I can send Little Dove or maybe someone will come into town in the morning," Anna answered. "We could still lose them both," she whispered as she looked at the women.

Liz gathered up her niece and sat in the rocker to feed her. "That won't be happening," she firmly stated.

Abby saw Liz's lips turn to a quiet, but persistent, prayer.

"Jackson…" Megan mumbled in her troubled sleep.

Chapter 5

Liz's only son, Luke, had grown into a handsome young man with his sun-streaked hair and Southern-gentleman-now-turned-Texan ways. He was quick to say, "Yes, ma'am" or "No, sir" or he would simply get the job done with no comment at all.

He had a healthy respect for Thomas, the man who had married his mother, sired his two feisty little sisters and had built a fine ranch in the hills of North Texas. Though Luke seldom thought about the loss of his dad, who had died when he was just a kid, he did think about his grandfather, Lucas Mailly, almost daily. Luke found it hard to think about his grandfather's old horse Millie being in the pasture every day. But that is where he knew she needed to be very soon. The horse loved the ranching life, but Luke knew the work was too demanding for the beloved mare. The growing ranch placed greater demands on both the men and the horses.

Luke rested easy in the saddle as he watched the sun start to creep up on the chilly morning. Dawn was always the coldest part of the day, and Luke pulled his collar up over his neck and ears and pushed his almost too-long, blonde hair inside. He had already been in his saddle for hours, riding the open countryside and watching the day unfold before him. He greeted the new day from his favorite spot, listening to the creak of the leather under him as he shifted his weight.

The longhorns were quiet and standing close together as they often did on cold nights. They hadn't yet started to warm up enough to graze. The newborn calves of the past week were huddled under their mothers. All were safe and accounted for under the watchful eyes of Luke and Bear, who barked as Luke urged his horse forward and started around the herd again. "We didn't lose any calves last night, Bear!" Luke patted Millie as a cold mist blew from her velvet nose.

Feeling the sun beginning to warm his face, he reached into the pocket of his sheepskin coat and pulled out a worn piece of paper to read it once again.

WANTED

Riders for the Pony Express!
Strong, wiry young men, light as jockeys
Weighing less than 125 pounds
$100 – $150 per month and found [room and board]

First-Class Stock
$150 – $250 a head

Luke felt a stir of honor at the thought of having a part in the founding of a mail service delivery from coast to coast. Two years earlier, he had finished his schooling and was happy to be a part of the family ranching business. Riding across the landscape everyday with Millie and Bear was wonderful. He felt that he was living his dream. He looked forward each day to the life of a cowboy. Owning a ranch, taking the raw land and turning it into something productive was appealing to him. Luke had watched Thomas in his various roles as a rancher, a cowboy, a family man, and a businessman taking part in shaping the politics of the West. For Luke to adapt to the cowboy code of hospitality, respectfulness, manners and hard work was effortless. He could easily see himself in the role of a rancher.

This place was unbelievably huge—where horses ran wild, fat cattle roamed free and rich black soil awaited planting. Streams ran clear and were brimming with fish. Luke was a Texan through and through—fiercely proud and independent like every other Texan.

But joining the Pony Express would be an adventure, a once-in-a-lifetime opportunity. He would tell his mom and Thomas as soon as he could. Luke Bromont would ride for the Pony Express.

With the sun at his back, Luke looked over the ridge and saw Chet riding his way. Luke had known Chet all of his life and had always looked up to him. Chet was almost family; he had worked at the family timber mill in Louisiana and had scouted for their wagon train when they came to Texas. He was a native-born Texan whose parents were part of the original 300 settlers who had moved to Texas over thirty years earlier. Stephen F. Austin had worked tirelessly with the Mexican government to receive the rights for a special backbreaking type of frontier family to renounce their American citizenship and carve out homes in Mexico's Indian Territory. Chet's family had received over 4,000 acres for grazing land close to the Brazos River. His dad had even fought at Goliad and died in the war with Mexico.

Luke's mom, Liz, and his grandfather had always trusted this man with his long, blonde hair and chocolate-brown eyes. They had spent a lot of time together over the years. With no brothers, Luke considered Chet to be as close as any blood bond could be. The Texan had schooled Luke in riding, ranching and cowboy etiquette as well as teaching him to speak Spanish.

"Hey, no action last night?" Chet asked as he rode closer.

"No, pretty quiet, just cold. Do you have the fire up and a coffee pot on it yet?"

"Yeah, should be ready by the time you get over there."

Chet paused and looked at his friend. "Luke?"

"Yeah? What?"

"I found some pretty big cougar tracks over on the ridge. I think that's what is getting our calves. From looking at the tracks, looks like one foot is injured or something."

"I'm sure Thomas will have us go out right away to find him while the trail is fresh…and before he has any more meals, thanks to us. I sure thought it was a pack of wolves."

Luke glanced toward a thicket of brush and trees. "Plenty of deer…sure wish he would eat them and leave our livestock alone."

"If he's hurt, all these calves makes it easy for him. Might even be a female with a batch of little ones."

"Jackson or Clyde or one of the other hands will be here anytime, and we will see what they want us to do. We'll get some supplies and head out."

Luke ambled to the campfire and poured a cup of coffee to warm his bones. He guessed he would head to the house for his hunting gear. *It'll be mid-morning before I reach the ranch house, and I'm already hungry as a wolf.*

Luke loved riding up and seeing the two-story house his mother had helped design with its sprawling wraparound porch. The building was nestled among a group of red oak trees with hen houses, barns, sheds and corrals placed neatly nearby. Mattie and Sofie's playhouse, painted pink, stood to the left of the back porch steps. *It's sure quiet when Liz and the girls are in town. Yep, I'll miss those cute little sisters of mine,* he mused.

Luke spotted Thomas and Buck at the corrals and headed in that direction, even though he could smell food coming from the house. He had been out several days and was plumb starved to death. Luke had a hard time not going to the house first for some of Lulu's great cooking. With Liz away half the week, a Mexican cook had been hired to help in the house. Her husband Poncho looked after the barns, corrals, chickens and hogs. Lulu and Poncho lived in the first house Thomas had built on the ranch—a small cabin behind the barn. How Liz had loved that cabin nestled among the oak trees.

At the corrals, Luke jumped from Millie's back, not even bothering to tie her up. She wasn't going anywhere anyway; after all, she already knew the routine. Though he loved the aging horse he had gotten from his great-grandfather, he had already decided to leave her at the ranch when he left.

He noticed that Thomas was intent on the action in the corrals. He saw Buck dust off his chaps and attempt to mount a shiny, black animal again. The stamping, snorting horse circled around the cowboy, rearing up while Buck pulled on the reins, displaying the fact he had more stamina than the man.

"Hey, Thomas," Luke called as he leaned on the fence.

"Good morning, Luke. How did it go out there?"

"Good. We haven't lost any calves since we started all-night guard duty."

Buck was back on the piece of lightning as the stallion circled the corral, kicking, twisting, bucking and snorting. Buck managed to ride him for a bit and then took to the dirt again. The horse stood close by, eyeing the man, seeming to dare him to remount.

"That horse has a mind of its own," Luke noted.

"Yep. Been on him thirty times a day for twenty-eight days, and he's still not taking a liking to it," Thomas said with a respecting tone.

"What will you do with him when he is broke?" Luke asked.

"Not sure. Probably look for a buyer."

"I would take him…been thinking of resting ol' Millie here." Luke continued to watch the horse, thinking he would name him *Thunder*.

"Might be a good match, Luke. I'll think on it."

Jackson rode in from the north and stopped his stallion, Zeus, at the corral. Little mud clods from a nearby puddle skittered from Zeus' hooves as they gripped in to make the quick stop.

"Met up with Chet, and he told me about the cat getting the calves. I want to go out with Chet to get him. They found prints on the ridge."

Jackson watched Thunder throw Buck yet again.

"Whew! What a pony!"

They heard Buck mutter a few choice words, and they watched him get ready to mount again. The horse neighed and pawed the ground, defying the annoying bronco rider.

Luke shared with Thomas and Jackson what little he knew about the cougar. Thomas listened carefully to what his men had to say about the losses in his herd. With the culprit responsible now identified and close at hand, a decision was quickly made regarding what needed to be done.

Thomas began issuing orders. "Luke, get your breakfast. Jackson, get our gear and pack some fresh supplies, and we'll go get Chet. Maybe, just maybe, we can find that cat before the trail grows cold." He wished Buck good luck with the stallion and went to saddle up.

With their hats pulled low to shield their faces from the noonday sun, each man rode tall in his saddle with the deep heel of his boot settled firmly against the stirrups of his high-backed, comfortable saddle. Their spurs jingled as their ponies loped across the rolling hills toward the herd. The horses enjoyed the run and stretched out with each stride to almost a full gallop. Their manes danced like fringe, their muscled bodies rippled and their tails arched and flowed with their growing speed. Hooves pounded the earth with confidence and sure footing.

Not a word was spoken as each man clearly focused on the task at hand. Leather chaps flapped in the breeze, protecting them from the mesquite and cactus thorns as they pushed past the thicket and up through a rocky ravine.

Jackson reached the top first and pointed to where the herd grazed. His horse Zeus shook his head and pranced impatiently. He waved to catch Chet's eye and then motioned for him to join the hunting party. Chet waved back and stomped out the coffee fire. He stowed the coffee pot and tin cup in his saddle bag, and in one smooth motion, he swung up on his horse Tootsie. As Chet settled in the saddle and glanced back over the herd, his horse circled a few times, her tail twitching with excitement. Rider and pony charged up the hill to the waiting cowboys. Thomas checked his hemp lariat fastened on the side of his saddle as he slowed a bit to look over the herd. His rope wasn't broken in yet, and the thought bothered him.

The four men rode to the ridge where the tracks had been last spotted. They continued to track the cougar all day. Several times, they were so close that the horses could smell the danger and resisted going forward. Confused by the fact that the cougar tracks were now overlapping, the hunters decided to make camp in a narrow canyon. Part of the area was protected by an overhanging rock ledge which would hold the heat from the fire. The nights were still chilly, and a little extra warmth would be appreciated by all four men.

"This cat is hard to figure." Chet shook his head as he rubbed his gloved hands close to the fire.

"Must be a female!" Jackson chuckled and set the perked coffee on a rock to the side of the campfire. A breeze tunneled through the wind-hollowed overhang, taking the warmth and smoke with it.

Luke leaned back to the rock wall, content to listen to the men and the occasional whistle of the wind. Chet passed him a tin of hot coffee.

The horses stood still. Suddenly, each head rose, nostrils flared and ears pricked to attention in an effort to detect the location of the looming danger. Zeus tossed his head and yanked on the rope where all of the horses were tethered at the edge of the ridge. The whites of his eyes were frightful as he tugged at the rope again.

Jackson stood to calm the ponies and peered into the dusky evening. "So are we the hunters or the hunted?" Jackson asked as he ran his hand over Zeus, soothing him. He spoke softly to calm the animal.

Thomas joined him in calming the other animals and checking the hitch knots. He didn't want the horses to get spooked and run away.

"Chet, didn't we do this once before?" Thomas asked with a hint of hesitance.

"Yeah, he stalked us for several days, I think. He never did show his face; that cat was doing it for fun," Chet replied as he built up the fire by adding a twisted oak branch. He had been poking at the fire with it and now watched the dry bark spark into a blue flame.

Luke opened a bag Lulu had sent with him. "Let's eat this before the cat eats us."

Thomas turned back to the fire. "Luke, I swear your belly has a hole in it!"

"I think the cat is a female, Jackson. Just when you think you are doing the hunting, you realize you are the one being hunted. Trapped—trapped like a wild animal, wide-eyed and scared for your life." Chet looked seriously at the fellows, as they laughed at him. It was even funnier because he was so serious and correct about the situation.

"Chet, who has you caged?" Jackson asked, knowing that Chet was sweet on Emma.

"That Emma. I don't get it. Talks to me, feeds me, okay with seeing me on the weekends, and even sits with me at church on Sunday. Then I see her being all nice with a new cowboy in town. Just happened to be pickin' some things up early in the week at the Mercantile, and there she was, pretty as you please, being all sweet with some yayhoo."

Luke chuckled around his third biscuit. They were almost as good as Emma's. He waited for Chet to pick up the last piece of chicken.

Thomas had been drinking coffee when Chet had begun his rant about being trapped by females and started laughing with a mouthful. Some of the hot liquid had gone down his windpipe, and he began coughing, choking and sputtering. "Has Miss Emma made it clear that she wants to settle down with you?" Thomas finally managed to choke out.

"No!" Chet replied, exasperated. "That's just it. We were both satisfied with our arrangement. Emma doesn't want to marry yet, and I don't want to set up housekeeping either. But I didn't expect her to go flirtin' around with other cowboys." He poked the fire again. "Caged! That's what I am. Why did she have to go and spoil it?"

Luke took a seat by his friend. *I've never seen him like this and all...over a girl!* He decided right then that the Pony Express was perfect for him. *No women in a two-thousand-mile territory will drag me down and tangle up my thinking. Just wide, open spaces with my horse and the wind at my back, passing a mail pouch from my pony to the next!*

In the four years they had lived in Texas, Luke had seen his family and friends pair up like Noah's ark before the flood. Babies were bursting forth like the rains that carried away the ark. *Yep, I'll be heading out pretty soon for the Overland Express.*

Jackson, confused over Chet's situation, also took a seat by Chet.

"Now don't get all worked up about this. Emma is sensible. I don't see her taking up with anyone. You said she wasn't looking to get married. Think about it, Chet! She feeds every cowboy in a 50-mile stretch."

"But that's just it!" Chet sighed. "She is forcing me to show my hand. Lay the law down that she's mine. That means a more permanent decision."

"I haven't heard my matchmaker wife mention any of this. If Emma were playing you, wouldn't Megan know…or even Liz? Thomas, has Liz said anything to you? You would have to know, right?" Jackson was trying to figure this out, worried about his buddy.

Chet looked to Thomas for the answer.

Thomas raised his hand in defense. "Sorry, I'm not privy to any information. But Chet, your intentions for Miss Emma need to be made known to me, as the man of this family and your boss." Thomas smiled and chuckled, hoping to ease the tension-filled atmosphere.

Jackson pulled a piece of chicken from the bone with his teeth. "Yeah, Chet, it must be horrible to have Thomas as your boss as well as the king of the Mailly harem."

Now that the matter of women seemed to be settled according to Luke, he asked, "So what's the plan for the cougar hunt and that last piece of Lulu's chicken?"

Chapter 6

For the next two days, the men hunted the cougar, and the cougar hunted them. The cat would lead them on and then double back to follow them. Each morning, they found where the cat had bedded down close to their camp. Their first night on the ridge, the cougar had slept on the cliff above them, watching their every move.

The cat they were tracking was a big mountain lion. The stride and paw prints were the largest any of the men had seen or heard of. Counting the lion's long tail, the cat measured an easy eight or nine feet long. By his tracks, the animal seemed to have a limp that bothered him none in his swagger. That paw must have been in a trap at some time, and the cat had still managed to escape.

Three times they had cornered him, and three times the cat had outsmarted and outrun the hunters. A respect was building among the men for the cougar's prowess.

As Thomas mounted his horse on the third morning, he declared, "If we don't get this cat, it will come back for the herd. Respect or not for this creature, we have to get it. Today. I'm not messing around."

Chet walked his horse a ways, checking the tracks. His pursuit certain, he commented, "You are the one I'm gonna get today." He stood, checked his favorite weapon, and was satisfied the pistol was loaded and ready.

Jackson tightened his saddle and shoved his Winchester into the saddle scabbard. "Zeus…" Jackson drawled as he punched a bullet into the chamber of his Colt revolver, "be ready for the big cat today. Gonna be a shootout."

Within the hour, the men finally had the cat cornered on a rocky edge. Knowing the cunning nature of the animal, they expected his usual tricks of escape. Luke and Thomas went to the left with Jackson and Chet cutting right.

Hollowed-eyed, the cat swayed to the left and then unexpectedly whipped around to the center. A glint of implacability filled the animal's eyes as it leaped over a fallen tree from the ledge. In one last attempt to free itself from the encircling men, the cat clawed at the rocks and gravel as it leaped toward them.

Luke snapped a shot from the hip with his rifle, only nipping the cat. Jackson, with a clear shot, ripped a round into the chest of the magnificent creature. When the smoke cleared, the cougar was no match against four men with guns.

Stepping carefully over the rocks and branches, Thomas admired the beautiful animal. He pointed to the cat's front paw. "Looks like she's been in a trap before. Well, let's get some branches and build a traverse. No horse is gonna let this huge cat ride piggyback."

When they started toward home, the going was slow with pulling the big cat. Zeus was none too happy to have the animal behind him.

As the men reached the edge of the ranch, they saw Lulu hanging out the laundry. When she spotted them, she dropped the wet shirt into the basket and came running toward them. "Mister Jackson! Mister Jackson!" she cried in her Spanish accent, out of breath. "Miss Megan…she have her baby three days ago. Calling and calling for you. She had a hard time."

Jackson jumped from Zeus and ran to the corral for a fresh horse. Within minutes he was saddled, and only a trail of dust could be seen as he headed toward Fort Worth.

Ian Jackson wasn't a lawman as most of the Rangers were. The harshness and the ways of the land hadn't hardened his heart. Thinking of his Megan in pain and calling for him brought the six-foot-four man to his knees. *What was I thinking of...marrying that feisty, petite woman and having a family? If I lose her... Well, I can't even think of that. I had no business loving her and being the cause of her pain.*

The borrowed horse snorted as Jackson urged it on; dust lifted from the pounding of each hoof meeting the trail. The shaken man pushed his hat down firmly and ran his hand over his unshaven jaw. He leaned in closer to the neck of the horse and whispered encouragement to the animal while wiping his sweaty palm on his coarse pants leg.

The lawman-turned-cowboy's strong sense of justice could handle most any situation or gun like it was welded to him. That, along with his love of the open territory, was what had propelled him to become a Ranger. But now with Megan and baby, he would hang up his gun and be a dirt farmer if he had to. *If only they're both alive...*

Darkness had fallen, and the hour was well past supper when Jackson yanked the exhausted horse to a stop at the Mailly house. Several lamps burned inside, causing the house to glow with warmth.

The door opened before Jackson's boot pounded the first step. Abby had been watching for him and held the door open. Jackson's face reflected the trepidation he felt on the inside. He waited to hear. "They're okay, Jackson. Megan is sleeping, and Liz is with the baby. It's been real bad. We expected to lose them both. Today is the first day we have had some good signs. Megan finally took some solid food today and sat up a short while. Your baby girl had strength to cry today. Before you could hardly hear her. She sounded like a kitten mewing."

Jackson stood inside the door. "They're both alive?" he whispered.

His face was contorted with all of his pent-up emotions on the edge of tumbling out.

"Yes, Jackson," Abby gripped his strong shoulder, reassuringly. "Go see them." Abby felt sorry for the big man. She could feel his body shaking with worry.

Jackson stepped into the bedroom he shared with his wife and, in the low light, stared at Megan sleeping. He noted her pale face and long eyelashes. Her dark-blonde, shiny hair was loose and fell across her shoulders and pillow. *She looks like a child—a sweet, precious, innocent child.* His heart beat inside his chest until he thought it would burst.

The squeak of the rocker made him turn toward his daughter being cradled in Liz's arms.

"Jackson, come hold your little girl. She's been waiting to see her papa." Liz stood and held the pink-faced little girl up to the tall Ranger.

Her head fit into the palm of one hand and her bottom in the other. *She's the tiniest thing I've ever seen.* Her eyelashes fluttered like her mother's, and the deep-blue eyes opened. She had a button nose and a perfect mouth, like a rosebud. Her lips parted and a coo or a mew, he wasn't sure which, came out. Her lashes fluttered again as she looked straight up at him.

At that moment, Jackson melted into a sugary puddle, and he knew he would never be the same.

"Well, little lady," he gruffly whispered as he cleared his throat and swallowed. "You have caused your papa a big scare," he paused, adoring her. "Just what are we to name you?"

Megan opened her eyes to see the meeting of father and daughter for the first time. Her heart squeezed with love and pride as she watched. Jackson, her hero, was home. She could now relax and regain her strength.

Jackson continued to stare at the little bundle and her tiny bit of soft downy hair covering her head. He noticed that it shined when he held her just right in the lamp light.

"Hmmm," he whispered. "Lydia?" She opened her dark eyes and her rosebud of a mouth seemed to turn up at the corners. "Oh, you like Lydia?" He spoke softly to her, memorizing every part of her face. "My grandmother was Lydia Varine, a very special and sweet lady. How about you take her name?"

The baby stared back at the giant man holding her and arched her back. She wiggled back into the tight bundle of the quilt in which she was wrapped and contentedly closed her eyes. Jackson moved her gently to the curve of his arm. "I'll never let you go, Lydia. I'll always be here for you and your momma!"

Chapter 7

Luke couldn't believe he would be riding for the Pony Express. He would be one of the men connecting the East with the West by delivering mail on horseback. The plan was for forty riders to head east and forty west, connecting at stations every ten miles to change horses and pass a leather mochila filled with letters and newspapers. Ten days was all that was required to carry the mail over two thousand miles of open country. The riders would cross the Great Plains and Rocky Mountains from St. Joseph, Missouri, to Sacramento, California.

Luke reread his letter of acceptance from the Overland Express Company. The owners wanted him to start by April 3, 1860. In just a few weeks, he would be racing across the vastness of the Wyoming territory. His orders were to report to Division 3 where he would ride the route starting at Horseshoe Creek. He was expected to ride for at least 70 miles, sometimes as long as twenty hours on horseback. The rules required that he change horses every ten miles so he would ride at a consistent high speed.

The excitement inside him swelled. He would tell Thomas and his mother when she came home on Sunday. Luke knew the time had come for him to go, and he knew his mother and family would need a few days to adjust to his leaving. He was sure a party would be in the works to wish him well at his new job.

Like all of the other cowboys who worked at the ranch, Luke was paid a dollar a week. With the Pony Express, he would earn twenty-five dollars a week. He wasn't sure for what purpose he was saving his money, but at that rate, he would quickly have a nice nest egg.

Luke was dressed and ready as the sun came in his bedroom window. He snuffed out the lamp and took the stairs two at a time and headed toward the kitchen where Lulu was opening the oven door.

"Mr. Luke, you're up early," she greeted him in her sweet accent. The oven door was closed on her delicious biscuits as she cocked her head at him. "What are you up to? You look like your two mischievous sisters!" She smiled. "You have a secret. I have seen it with you for days."

Luke gulped as he realized Thomas was standing beyond the kitchen doorway, next to the hallway leading to his office. "Yeah, Luke. You have been up to something. First, I thought it was a girl, then the horse we are breaking, but now…" Thomas said as he rubbed the two-day growth on his chin.

Luke stopped dead in his tracks at the foot of the stairs. Lulu and Thomas both locked eyes on Luke. He couldn't take the secret any longer. *Maybe it would be best to tell Thomas first and then my mother later. Thomas can help soften the blow. Yeah, maybe this is best,* he thought.

"Well," Luke said as he sauntered toward the table and then gripped the back of one of the chairs. "Thomas, I've been thinking about riding for the Pony Express."

Lulu's jaw dropped in disbelief, and she glanced at Thomas. "Miss Liz gonna have a lot to say on this," she mumbled and clicked her tongue a few times.

Thomas stared at Luke, knowing she was right. *Liz will be a force to reckon with, but I'll hear the boy out.* "Luke, you can make your own choices here. But I thought you were happy ranching here at the Rolling M."

"Oh, I am. Make no mistake. I just got a hankering to do this." Luke paused and became serious with his stepdad. "Thomas, it's… it's history. It's a once-in-a-lifetime opportunity. I just feel like I have to do this."

Thomas could see the excitement and desire in the young man standing strong before him. "Have you corresponded with the outfit?"

Luke reached in his pocket to pull out the summons for riders and his letter of acceptance. He handed them to his boss.

Thomas read the papers, carefully evaluating the situation. He didn't want Luke to go for several reasons, but Thomas felt he couldn't tell him "No" either.

"So I guess you are telling me that you're quitting."

"Yes," Luke said as he swallowed hard and rubbed the stubble on his own chin. When Liz was away at the Mercantile in town, both Thomas and Luke refrained from using the razor. "I really like ranching, Thomas. Thank you for the work."

Thomas walked to the table and stood closer to Luke. "Do you want some help with your mother?" he asked as he handed the papers back to Luke.

Lulu stopped the watching and turned to the stove, mumbling, "Gonna be gone that day. Oh, Miss Liz not gonna like it—not one bit." She shook her head, mumbling to herself in Spanish and went to work scrambling the eggs.

Thomas chuckled at Lulu's self-talk until he saw the worry on Luke's face. The kitchen chair made a scraping noise as Luke pulled it out and dropped into it.

"No, no," he paused, gathering his thoughts and courage. "If I am man enough to ride, then I'm man enough to tell my mother."

Lulu looked over her shoulder at Luke and repeated more unintelligible Spanish words in her worried tone.

"She has her hands full, Luke, what with the girls and the mercantile and with Megan and little Lydia."

Luke looked at Thomas, wanting to believe him, but felt more inclined to believe Lulu at the moment.

"When do you want to tell her, and when do you leave? Do we have time to finish breaking Thunder for you?" Thomas wanted to get Luke thinking about the new journey and not his mother's reaction.

"I think she will do better if I give her a little time to prepare. Was thinking of telling her this week when she returns to the ranch. I need to head out as soon as possible." His eyes lit up as he spoke. "Thomas, they pay twenty-five dollars a week!"

"I sure can't compete with that." Thomas forked his eggs and took a big bite. Luke's excitement was contagious.

"They provide the horses for the rider, but I do need my own horse to get there and to get around on my own," Luke said as his thoughts turned to the Pony Express and momentarily forgot his mother. "I would really like to have Thunder. I've been in the corral with him quite a bit. I think we can get along. Jackson's been teaching me some Indian ways with him. Those Comanche braves really have a way with their ponies."

Lulu poured more coffee for the men and actually felt sorry for them. They didn't have a clue what was in store for them when Liz arrived home and heard the news.

Chapter 8

Liz didn't need a calendar to know that spring had arrived early to North Texas. The days were getting warm, and the plants were greening up with little buds waiting to pop out. She was at the place she loved most—sitting on the porch, watching her world. With her mending finished, she could start the piecing on her latest quilt, a Shoo-Fly design.

She had chosen a tobacco-brown for the large triangle in the block. After examining the piece of cloth in the sunlight, she thought the fabric contained a hint of green. She tied up the thread already in her needle and picked up a precut square from her favorite turkey-red. Tiny stars floated on the red print. She stopped to place the right sides together and then stitched along the imaginary quarter-inch seam allowance. Scraps saved from a beautiful, red floral Jacobean print used in her newest dress lay in her basket, waiting for their placement in her quilt.

She loved the piecing of the fabrics; the sound of the thread being pulled through the fabric was calming but exciting. The piecing was where color and design started to take shape. She could always imagine how the shapes and color would go together, but not until one block was stitched was it acceptable to continue on with the other blocks of the quilt. Liz always reserved the right to make changes as needed and never felt inalterable loyalty to what her mind had imagined it to be. She loved scrap quilts over all others as each block took on a life of its own with color and shape married to each other. Yes, piecing, above all other steps of quilt making was what she loved best. The freshly pressed and evenly stacked fabric shapes lay neatly in a shallow cheese box from the Mercantile, just waiting for the needle to assign them to their location.

She glanced up to see Princess, one of Callie's grown kittens, sunning her fatness on the porch. The purring, sleeping cat was due anytime with a litter of her own kittens.

Mattie and Sofie were playing in their pink playhouse, concocting mud pies. They giggled as a butterfly fluttered and floated on the breeze. Liz smiled and rested her needle as she watched her girls.

All was right and in place in her world. She loved to sit on the porch and stitch as it all passed before her. She prayed for her family one by one, thanking God for His blessings and asking for His help in anything that was lacking. With Megan and baby Lydia now gaining strength, her blessing list now went on forever. She praised and thanked her Creator for all He had bestowed upon them. The joy she felt in her heart was as much a part of her as the color of her hair. She thought of Nehemiah 8:10 and softly repeated the words of the verse as she pulled the needle through another patch. "...*The joy of the* LORD *is my strength.*" She did feel the energy of the intense emotion; it was a state of being that influenced her and gave her courage. She wanted to sing and even dance to praise God for allowing Megan and her baby to regain their strength. She had felt the deep, gut-wrenching pain of losing family, and her happiness on this day was as strong in the opposite direction. She stopped and wiped a tear of joy from her face.

"...*Take heart! I have overcome the world.*" The truth of this Scripture flowed through her thoughts. And it was true. They had sold the timber mill in Louisiana, traveled West by wagon train, found Fort Worth and had started a new life. She had put behind her the robbery of her mercantile and the death of her grandfather. She was surprised as to how long it had been since she had thought of Caleb, Luke's father. Yes, her son would have that look of his dad that sparked a thought, but her days were full of her little girls, the family, the work at the ranch and the Mercantile. She seldom had time to go looking into her past.

Her excitement and energy for life—this joy had allowed her to dream once again. Abby and Samuel were about to be married. The community was excited for the wedding day. Plans were taking place for a really grand celebration. Samuel had important friends coming from Austin, and the old Army barracks were being freshened up for the welcomed guests. She trusted the preparations would be enough as mistreating a guest in your home or community was a sin. *I don't want to let down my friends and family in any way.*

The city could fill up fairly quickly on a weekend as it was. The town still did not have a hotel. Some Saturday shoppers would stay over to Sunday morning to hear Pastor Parker preach and then eat at Emma's Table before heading back to their homestead. Town friends would open their homes or put fresh hay in the barn for the overnighters.

So for all of the wedding guests, extra rooms were required. They were already traveling several days to get here. They surely needed a more comfortable space while they were here. Liz would have offered her home and extra sleeping rooms if she weren't so far away from town and all of the wedding festivities.

Liz's prayers continued.

Megan had her new baby, and both parents were as taken as ever with the little girl. Jackson was never far and seldom took his eyes away from his two girls. Little Lydia was already wrapped around their hearts and the rest of the family as well. She was a good baby with no colic and already slept through most of the nights.

Emma was next in her thoughts and on her prayer list. She seemed fine—happy with her restaurant and chicken business. She didn't seem to be visiting her dark places and quiet thoughts. Only the other day she had heard Emma laughing as she stood in front of her store on the boarded sidewalk. Thomas had come home from the cougar hunt, asking about Emma and saying Chet was all out of sorts with something that had happened between the two. *Well, I'm not aware of any of it,* but she added their friend Chet to her prayers anyway. *Yes, Emma is fine,* Liz thought and picked up her needle again.

These are the moments for which I live. She pulled and pushed her needle, and the neat, even stitches nestled down in the fabric, not too tight, but just right. She ran two fingers across the stitches, admiring the crispness of her work. Liz thought about Luke and was puzzled. He had asked if he could talk with her and Thomas later in the afternoon. *Probably just wants to talk about the new horse or something about a ranch decision. With the herd growing and no predator killing the young ones, the ranch life had returned to normal.*

"Oh, stop it," she said out loud as a thought came to mind. Thinking back to something her grandfather Lucas always said, she repeated, "If things are good, enjoy it and thank God as troubles are coming your way. If things are bad, ask God for help and look forward as good times are coming back to you!"

Things are good! Liz didn't want her mind to wander to the negative side of what could be. Of course, the threat of war was always close to everyone's thoughts, but she pushed on through hers.

The dust behind the corral stirred, so she knew Luke was riding in on Thunder. Horse and rider made an impressive pair. The shiny coat of the dark horse rippled with the muscles of the spirited animal. His mane and tail ebbed and flowed with each gallop. Luke was lean with his weather-faded shirt tucked neatly into his pants. The shirt fit snugly over his toned chest and shoulders. The fringe of his leather chaps swung with each step of the horse. His hair was longer than she would have preferred and not yet too sun-streaked.

Thomas strolled toward her from the barn and headed to where she sat on the porch. Putting down her sewing, she thought, *He already knows what's on Luke's mind.* The two had been together for weeks while she had been spending time in town at the Mercantile and lately caring for her sister and baby Lydia. *Yes, I'm certain Thomas knows.* She watched her husband stop to wash his hands at a water crock, and soon Luke stopped to wash up too.

Mattie and Sofie ran to meet the two men. Thomas reached down to swing up the littlest girl while Luke took the other. He swung her in a wide circle as she squealed with delight.

"Would you like a bite of our chocolate cake?" the little girls teased as Bitty and Nancy, their Banty hens clucked past. The girls wiggled to get down and go after them.

Liz watched joyously as the two men sat the little girls down and walked up to the porch. She couldn't hear their talking over Luke's jingling spurs and her daughters' happy chatter.

Lulu appeared with glasses of fresh lemonade. Liz had unexpectedly received some lemons from down South and eagerly brought them home. A group of Mexicans, anxious to trade at her Mercantile, had bartered the lemons for some more staple food items. When Liz had placed them on the kitchen table, Lulu's eyes had lit up. She rattled something in Spanish Liz didn't understand, but she could tell her cook was excited to receive them. Lulu had hugged them to her chest and sighed, "Home." Liz smiled at her friend and housekeeper as her musings about the lemons quickly left her thoughts.

"Thank you, Lulu," Thomas said, interrupting her thoughts.

Lulu gave the two men a strange look as she quickly left the porch. Liz thought, *Lulu's acting strangely. Is she in on this too?* Before she could further form her thoughts, Luke started talking.

"Well, Mom, there's no way I can sugarcoat this. Neither of us likes to let things drag on." Luke leaned on the porch rail. He looked to Thomas, although he wasn't asking for help. He looked back at his mother. "I've been reading about it for a while now and even sent a letter. Thought about it long and hard."

Liz stared at her son and then quickly looked at Thomas. *Yes, he knows what's in my son's heart, and he's even given him the blessing. I can tell.* She put her sewing in her lap again and licked her lips. *I don't have a clue as to what my son has been thinking on.*

"They want riders for the Pony Express, and I'm going to go," Luke stated matter-of-factly.

Liz was stunned by his announcement; her mouthy fell open, and she had to tell herself to close it. He wasn't asking her permission, and she didn't need to give it. He was young, but still, he was a man who could make his own decision on his matters.

She looked to Thomas who stood quietly watching the exchange.

"Aren't you happy here?" she asked, wondering if he had concerns she wasn't privy to knowing.

"Yeah, it's a dream come true, and what Grandpa and I always talked about," he stated with excitement, "but…this is somethin' I gotta do. It's history, Ma." He smiled, and his face lit up with desire.

Liz bit the side of her lip. "Well, I guess it's decided then." Quietly, she asked, "When do they expect you to leave?"

Luke came closer and leaned on a knee at her chair. "It will be good, Ma. You'll see."

"I'll just miss you. Mattie and Sofie will miss you." Liz's eyes watered, and her voice tightened with emotion.

"Oh, Ma. Don't worry." Luke didn't want her to cry.

"Well," she straightened, trying to regain her composure, "how long do we have?"

"I need to go soon—really, as soon as I can. I've received a letter that tells me to report to Wyoming."

Liz blinked at Luke. "Wyoming," she stated quietly, the tears trickling down her cheeks. *Grandfather was right,* she thought. *It was just around the corner. It wasn't only around the corner but on her porch that very day.*

Chapter 9

Liz scowled as she read the letter from one of her suppliers. She tried to shake the thought about what Parker and Samuel had discussed earlier. The pit of Liz's stomach hurt as she turned away from the men, who were discussing the matter with each other in the Mercantile. Pastor Heath Parker took the Austin newspaper and scanned the story Samuel talked about.

"I don't understand," Parker stated, "how they can want the Southern cotton farmer to do anything different than what they are already doing? The rotation of the cotton money between the North and the South is as tightly woven together as a piece of cotton fabric. The Northern businessmen brought the slaves to the South in the first place. They had the ships and the money to bring the workers to the Caribbean and the Southern states of the Union. Then the slaves were sold to provide labor for growing tobacco, cotton and sugar cane. The North bought the raw goods, packed them on their ships and sailed to the manufacturers. The North made money at every turn, even again as European and Massachusetts' mills bought the raw cotton."

"And to top it all," Parker took a breather, "the finished goods were sold back to the wealthy families of the South along the Mississippi River!"

"Yes," Samuel agreed calmly, but firmly, "and 70 percent of that money stays with the Northern businessmen. But the South is being punished for holding slaves."

Heath Parker, confused and frustrated, shook his head. "This tangled web absolutely makes no sense to me."

Samuel stood in disbelief. "I know, but like it or not, this is where it is at. The spring political conventions are just a short time away. Those who are nominated to run in each party will tell us a lot." Samuel paused a moment to consider. "The coming election has me torn between disappointment and excitement. Our political parties are even in disarray. The new Republican Party will likely put Abraham Lincoln on their ballot. The Democrats are split—Northern Democrats and Southern Democrats—and they can't agree. The well-known Stephen Douglas will most likely be with the North, and the Southern Democrats will likely choose Breckenridge, even though he is a registered Independent."

Parker shook his head again as he listened and tried to follow what Samuel was saying. Samuel had political friends in Austin and knew more than anyone else in the area about the way the political arena was shaping up. "The third party," Samuel added, "is the Constitutional Union Party with John Bell. I cannot believe any solid Texan would vote for him." Samuel was still sour over Bell and his wishy-washy politics.

As both men pondered the situation, Liz knew the silence wouldn't be lengthy. She looked back and forth to each, wondering what would be said next. Because of being in the general store several days a week, she usually heard all of the news and opinions of the public. She valued the wisdom and truth of Samuel's comments as he always provided both sides of the issue. *Guess it's the lawyer in him,* she thought.

"This Abe Lincoln," Samuel started anew, "in general, I don't think he is against the South. He delivered a good speech on a house divided and spoke highly of the Union's staying together. He said no good can come of division. Sam Houston is very much against Texas leaving the Union. He agreed that nothing good will come of it. Seems some are just riled up for a fight, come thick or thin."

Liz watched the two go out the door and continue to talk on the wooden walk. She felt tension build through her arms, shoulders and the back of her neck. She wanted to know what else they were saying, but also knew it was best to get her mind off the issue. She sat at her desk to finish opening her mail as her sister came in the back door with Lydia. Megan settled in the rocking chair, adjusting the quilt on her blonde cupid.

"I just needed to get out while the sun was shining. I'm feeling so much more like myself." She heard Liz sigh. "What is it, Liz?" Megan questioned, as she contentedly rocked and began nursing her little Lydia Varine. She couldn't help but notice Liz's uneasiness as she rubbed the knot at the base of her neck.

"Some of the supplies for the Mercantile are going to be in short order."

Megan looked at her sister, silently asking why.

"This separation of the North and South is growing stronger each day. Seems that some of the things we order will take longer or cost more because the Southern suppliers aren't shipping with the North and vice versa. With the transcontinental railway of the South being the only way of transport and with a boycott of Northern goods, we just can't purchase some things. My last order of cotton yard goods will now cost my customers four dollars a yard."

Megan listened and patted her baby on the back. A dainty burp was heard, and Megan smiled at the baby. "Four dollars a yard?" Megan repeated, letting the cost soak in. "Who could possibly afford a new dress at that price?"

Liz shrugged her shoulders as Megan repeated the statement.

Threads of Courage

Then Liz added, "Some new weaving and garment sewing mills will be opening in the South any day. Hopefully, their opening will help with the price of yard goods and ready-made goods."

"What do you think is ahead for us? What would Grandpa say?" Megan asked as she rocked her satisfied bundle to sleep. She remained calm, but was still very concerned.

Liz listened to the comforting creak of the wooden rocker as Megan rocked back and forth. She found it hard to remain calm as she read the newspaper stories each week and listened to the talk in her store.

"The North continues to look down their noses at the romanticized plantation life, not realizing that the majority of farmers and ranchers cannot afford to purchase, feed, and house a bought man. The cavalier days and chivalry is a jarring contrast to Northern society. The unrest is economic and social," Liz explained to her sister as they sat in the small office of the general store. "I think a Civil War will come just as Grandpa predicted." With a somber look, her eyes met Megan's. "We can only be wise in our actions and decisions and pray for the good Lord to protect us. That's all any of us can do."

"What about our men folk?" Megan asked. "What do you think Texas will decide?"

"Wisdom and protection for all of us, Megan. God already knows, and He has written over and over again in the Scripture that He is our protection and Provider and that we have power with His name."

Megan knew what her sister preached, but she wasn't sure that her words of assurance comforted her as well as she would have liked. She looked down at her innocent baby and kissed her cheek.

"We already left the deep South where we knew it would be dangerous. We listened and obeyed. I hope Texas won't need to choose sides. The statesmen in Austin want state's rights. But the governor is advocating to stay with the Union," Liz repeated, "even our state has two opinions."

Back to her spirited self, Megan replied, "Well, Liz, the North needs to take a long look in their own backyards. The moral issue of Southern slavery doesn't hold a candle to their sweatshops and child labor in their industrial factories. Those dresses we order come from a different type of slavery. The North works those laborers to death with no food, long hours and horrible living conditions. They prey upon the immigrants; when one dies they simply replace him without a second thought. At least the plantation owners have money invested with their slaves and want them to live. Besides, most Southerners are too poor to own slaves. This problem isn't going to be solved in our parlors or by our statesmen swirling their bourbon. They are as confused as the whole nation is as to what to do. The South is confident to a fault, and the North is persistent and vocal."

Megan hit the nail on the head and summed up the issue fairly quickly, Liz thought.

Lydia fidgeted at the emphasis of her mother's storm of words. Megan rocked and patted with less firmness, and the baby settled back into her sleep. She looked to her sister, who sat silently lost in thought.

"What is it, Liz? Is there more I don't know?"

As Liz glanced at her sister, sadness filled her face. *I feel like my world is ripping apart. Just a few days ago I was feeling so blessed and content on my porch, and then Luke said he was leaving. Everything is in a state of unrest.* She hadn't slept the past few nights. She knew she needed to turn to prayer but hadn't yet released the burden.

She sighed. "Luke has decided to ride for the Pony Express. He will head north to Wyoming Territory any day. I asked him to wait for Abby's wedding. Thunder is finally broken, and Luke will take him when he goes." She paused, pulling together all of her thoughts and emotions. "Megan, I always thought he would stay on at the ranch. He was so happy there."

Megan silently looked down at her sleeping beauty. She couldn't bear the thought of Lydia's ever leaving home. Tears quickly welled in her eyes at the thought and for her sister.

As the day wore away, the sisters went their separate ways, but their thoughts continued along the path of change. They couldn't shake their feelings of uncertainty. That evening, the crickets sang their usual comforting lullaby—a sharp contrast to the matter on everyone's mind. The nation was coming unhinged, and though everyone was aware of it, they felt completely helpless to stop it.

Chapter 10

Sally sat on the school steps, smiling brightly about the two dollars in coins she was holding tightly in her hand. Her lunch pail was open, and she quickly swallowed something from the contents inside it.

Sitting next to Sally, Odessa asked, "So how did you earn that much money?"

"That man that Momma works for gave it to me to keep. He said he knew that I never got any money. That I just helped Momma."

"She washes clothes?" Odessa asked, still not opening her lunch pail and thinking about the money. She sat holding her hair away from her face as the wind whipped up around them.

"Ya, first you have to set up the tub on a hot fire so the smoke won't get in your eyes. Then you put water in the tub. Since it rained some, we have rainwater close. But sometimes I have to haul water from the crick behind the house. I also shave the soap for the hot water and sort piles of clothing for Momma.

"After the water is boiling hot, she rubs the clothes on the rub board 'til her hands are raw. I tried it once; it hurts. She told me she would do all of that. She puts it in the tub and stirs it with an old broom handle. I hang the clean shirts on the line, rags and towels on the fence. I scrub the porch with the hot, soapy wash water when we are done with it. When we're finished, we pour the rest of the rinse water in the neighbor's flowerbeds. She has rose bushes, but we don't have any flowers at our place."

Threads of Courage

Odessa put a piece of bread in her mouth and looked at Sally as she described her responsibilities in detail.

"That's a lot of money. Whatcha gonna do with it?"

"Not sure. Never had any money to spend."

Abby stepped to the doorway to call the students back inside. She wanted to finish her teaching day a little early. The time had come to make her final wedding preparations. In a few days, she would be Mrs. Samuel Smith.

Just as Abby collected her last student, a wagon came barreling into town as if pushed by the wind.

"Fire! Fire!" the driver yelled. "Prairie fire! Teacher, ring the bell! Ring the bell!" Abby pulled on the bell for what seemed like several minutes before Samuel came to relieve her aching arms.

Abby didn't know the man announcing the fire; he was a newcomer. She thought he had a place out by Mrs. Perkins. Maybe he had even bought some of her ranch land a while back.

Frantic, he barked out, "The fire took my house and barn and some of my livestock. It got the Perkins' place too. Has anyone seen Mrs. Perkins? I couldn't find her. The fire…The fire…the fire was blazing all around. The wind was so strong. It wasn't there, and then it reared up and roared right in front of you. Her place was smoking and crumbling down."

Abby couldn't believe what she was hearing. By now, a large crowd had gathered at the school. Everyone looked afraid and didn't know what to do as they listened to the man's report in horror.

"What do we do?" one man yelled out.

"What started it?" another shouted.

"Is it coming toward town?" Liz asked, looking for smoke in the sky and which way the wind was headed. All she saw were a few storm clouds out Mrs. Perkins' way, but she noticed the wind was blowing with even more strength. Samuel stepped up on the school porch and looked over the crowd. Panic was written on each face. He knew that the town didn't stand a chance if the adults panicked or froze. He thought quickly to organize and put control into action as he started to call out some orders.

"Beat down any weeds around your houses and barns and buildings. Look for anything that could fuel the fire. Haul water and wet down your property good. Put wet tow sacks on your roofs. Secure your animals. If the fire gets close, turn them all loose. Don't wait too long. Hurry! Time is not on our side. Looks like the storm and the wind are heading in our direction."

People scattered in all directions to follow Samuel's suggestions. No one spoke; they simply went to their work of fighting a raging prairie fire where a life and a life's work could be lost in moments. Not only was the work gone, but nothing would remain to even hold to remind people of what had been.

Abby instructed all of the country kids to go help Samuel in town. She certainly couldn't send them home with the fire looming ever closer. She then sent the town kids to their homes to warn and to help their own families. Samuel kissed Abby on the cheek and hurried down the steps.

"It's gonna be okay," he shouted back. "Run and help Megan and Emma; check on the little ones. Secure the house as best you can and stay alert. Prairie fires can be a beast." Samuel quickly ran down to the livery to get his horse. He wanted to see where the fire had been, find out about Mrs. Perkins and check on his other neighbors.

❀ ❀ ❀

Samuel rode behind the fire as far as he could before his horse wouldn't go any farther into the burned area. Finally understanding the horse was scared and a hindrance, he slid down to the blackened soil with smoke trails still rising from the scorched earth all over the prairie. As his eyes adjusted to the stinging smoke, what he saw looked like the pit of hell—dead, smoldering animals, including cattle, horses, deer and many small, formerly furry creatures—lay scattered, caught in their hopeless flight to safety. He shook his head to remove the picture he saw and sighed. Turning his back on the devastated prairie, he removed all of the bullets from his saddlebags, tucked the extra revolver into his belt, and pulled the rifle from its scabbard. He grabbed his cartridge belt and slung it over his head to rest crosswise across his chest like a bandolier. He patted the rump of his horse, and it trotted away. He turned and slowly walked into the chamber of death. He had never seen such a sight. As far as his eyes could see, the carnage smoked around him.

Samuel saw three frightened horses running, but going nowhere. As he approached them, they slowed and stood waiting for his approach. "Whoa, boy," he spoke calmly, soothing them and approaching slowly. Responding, they nickered and welcomed him. He didn't touch them but continued to talk in soothing tones as he walked around them, inspecting their deep burns. When he realized that all three had been blinded in the fire, he backed away, lifted his rifle and took aim. As he reloaded, he heaved and wiped his face of tears and soot with his sleeve. Taking aim again, the last horse fell. "Sorry, little ponies, you fought the fire and won, but you can't survive like this," Samuel said out loud as if to ease his conscience. He rested his rifle on his shoulder and walked on.

With a mile or so behind him, he saw a herd of deer fleeing from the fire and running toward a thicket and group of trees where they would normally find safety. However, in their flight from the fire, they were literally on fire, running and jumping, attempting to escape from the flaming predator on their backs.

Samuel knew the Tate ranch was just ahead. He saw a line of smoke, and a blaze already starting where the animals had been. *I can't let these running torches set the woods on fire!* Raising his gun to his shoulder, he took aim and fired multiple times, shooting those closest to the forest first. The sound of another gun rang out, and Mr. Tate was suddenly with him, shooting at the small herd as they leaped to their doom.

When the last of the deer was finally down, Samuel asked, "You looking for some of your horses?"

"Yes, I let a group go when I thought the fire was turning toward our place." He looked at Samuel, hoping to hear they had escaped.

"A bay and two light-colored ones?" Samuel asked without hope in his voice.

"Yes," Mr. Tate answered.

"They were blinded by the fire."

Tate's shoulders dropped, understanding the bad news.

"Sorry, friend, I thought best to put them down."

"Ya, thank you, Samuel. It is for the best."

Samuel placed his hand on his friend's back, "How's your family and the rest of your place?"

Obviously weary, Mr. Tate looked up, gathering strength from his friend. "Alive…" was all he had the courage or strength to get out. The two walked on together, and for the rest of the night hours, they continued to put down the wounded and dying animals left in the wake of the fire. They walked from ranch to ranch, checking on their friends whom the fire had hit first. The aftermath was more than any had seen before; the ones left alive were lucky to be breathing.

By dark, the citizens of Fort Worth were tired and hungry but continued to fight through the night. They fought the towering wall of fire as it swept dangerously close to the town. The glow of the fire that made a frightful sight against the blackness of the night sky went as far as the eye could see in any direction. The flames seemed to dance up and down as if set to music. A strange melody came from the blaze as twigs and branches sizzled and popped to an eerie, haunting tune.

Megan stood on the porch with Abby and Emma, watching the range glow in an angry flame. The sight and smell of smoke surrounded them. "Has Mrs. Perkins been found yet?"

"No," Emma choked, staring at the orange glow in the sky. "The wind has shifted again and moved the fire away from town. Samuel went around behind the fire and headed to her place. It will take him a while to get there. I don't expect him back anytime soon."

"Do we know if the Rolling M or the Longmonts' ranch were ever in danger?" Megan asked, thinking about her sister's place where Jackson would be and her friend Katie and her family.

"Mostly those south and west of town were in the path of the fire. The Turners got a little fire, and the Tates fought it pretty hard. Old man Graham's place was destroyed again," Emma replied somberly.

"I've never seen anything like this." Abby quietly leaned on the porch rail as smoke drifted across a sliver of the moon. "Do we dare close our eyes to sleep? Has the danger passed?"

Emma stood like a soldier with soot smeared on her face and apron. Emma had fought to save her side of Main Street with her restaurant and Liz's Mercantile. She had carried wet tow sacks up a ladder to the roof line. Her hands were red, and her shoulders felt ripped from her body. She had quickly dug a dirt trench around her chicken houses and gotten most of her hens in the coops before the fire shifted in her direction, endangering all she that loved and owned. The hungry flames moved so swiftly as the wind pushed them in one direction and then the other. The wildfire was headed straight toward her, looking for even more victims when Megan cried, "God, please help us!" Suddenly, the flames altered direction toward the edge of the orchard as it swung again, only crisping a few trees and scampering toward the creek where that part of the fire rapidly died.

"You two go ahead. I'm up for the night. Liz is on the other side of town watching, and I'll stay here and watch."

Lydia started to cry softly. *She's hungry again.* Megan went inside and picked up the baby. She whispered a prayer over Mattie and Sofie as they slept with angelic-looking faces, unaware of the sinister danger snaking its way across the prairie. The night had gone by so quickly. She dreaded the dawn, which would reveal the extent of the damage and the buildings burned and destroyed by the ravaging, glowing demon.

Shortly before dawn, Liz urged her horse forward along the edge of town. Her hair was full of smoke and even her braid was sooty, with more loose hairs than braided blonde strands. Every muscle in her body ached, and she felt sure her shoulders were no longer attached to her body. She glanced down at her dress that now had singed holes in several places. She thought about the battle she had waged into the night. She had lost her bonnet early on in the evening as she steadily beat out fires with a wet tow sack, watching them spark and sizzle into nothing.

Once when the fire had crept upon her in the night, catching the hem of her dress on fire as she beat at the beast, she had thought to jump into a horse tank to put out the fire. She stopped when she realized she would be weighed down by the water and less capable of fighting the fires. Instead, she had soaked the burning edges of her skirt in the trough. She had then reached down to pull the now muddy, filthy and ragged hemline from the back of her full dress up to the waistband in the front and firmly tucked in the full skirt. She was now wearing what looked like a loose-fitting pair of pants.

Liz and the others had beaten the fire away from several buildings in town just as their prayers were answered, and the wind shifted. She had never before experienced anything as violent as this raging inferno. The wildfire had appeared out of nowhere and had devoured everything in its path, turning and twisting with a wicked, bright-orange gracefulness. Never stopping to regroup, building with power and heat, the wildfire moved like a monster over its unsuspecting prey.

Fire seemed so uncontrollable to Liz. *You never know when it will show up or how it will take the things you love.* She had experienced the heartbreak of fire before; a fire had taken the lives of her parents when she and Megan were only little girls. The house had caught fire late one evening. She, Megan, and an appliquéd quilt of her grandmother's were all that remained of the wreckage. That quilt had now survived three fires that took everything in their path. The first fire that took Mr. Graham's house wasn't all that long ago. Fire was an everyday worry for everyone, and the pioneering families certainly took the matter seriously.

Where had this one come from? How did it start? she wondered. She stopped for a moment as the last orange trail flickered out. She looked around, and this time she saw no fires. All through the night, the sky had been lit up in shades of orange, red and blue fire trails. Now she saw only darkness and smelled the pungent odor of smoke. If any fire remained, it had fled on past them, preying upon new victims and whatever came in its pathway.

Her hands were sore and sooty. Everything about her was in smelly disarray. Her eyes felt burned from the heat. She realized she ached from the top of her head to the toes of her black boots. Out of nowhere, the horse that she had lost during the night nuzzled up against her. Looking over the horse for any injuries, Liz realized he seemed to be in good shape. "Where have you been?" she asked in amazement. "Have you come for comfort or to take this weary body home?" Liz actually thought she heard her body creak as she wearily pulled herself into the saddle still on the back of the horse, hoping the animal would take her home.

As Liz wearily rode toward home, she thought about her fear of fire. This was now the second time that fire had threatened her life, and this time she wasn't a little girl. She didn't stand by in fear and watch it steal her beloved family from her. This time she had stood resolutely against the implacable foe, fighting with all she had to keep what was hers. *My family is safe. Thank You, God.* Their livelihood was intact. In the morning she would see how the rest of the community had fared in their battles. She hated the thought of fire, but this time, on this day, she had won!

Needing to rest her burning eyes, she lay back over the saddle's cantle and rested her head on the horse's rump and began to pray. The horse continued to walk slowly toward the Mailly house on the other side of town. When Liz arrived at the house, Emma came hurrying to help her exhausted cousin dismount from the horse. Liz didn't remember much except that the sky lit up with cloud-to-ground flashes of lightning as rain started to pound the charred, bleak earth. *Rain is always welcome; lightning is not!*

Chapter 11

Fort Worth had grown into a close-knit community where ranchers and townspeople gave freely to each other. In times of need, they banded together; and in times of plenty, they shared voluntarily of their time and talent and treasure. Mrs. Perkins was the one who had started it all. When the Mailly women arrived in town, started the school, and opened the general store, Mrs. Perkins could really see the town taking shape. She did everything in her power to welcome all of the newcomers and help those in need. Her husband had died years earlier when they were about the only ones around. They had fought Indians and snakes to make a home. With their only daughter living in Georgia, Mrs. Perkins had adopted everyone as her family, whether or not the person wanted to be adopted. Loving all the people with whom she came in contact was her way of life.

Abby and Samuel sat quietly together on the porch. His arm rested on the back of the bench behind her shoulders as they gazed at the black, sooty earth, all molten together after the heavy rains. Unable to express in words what they felt, their mood was very somber. At least, the rain had washed away the lingering smell of smoke. The sunshine of the day helped push the memories of the past few days further away.

Abby sniffled. "I can't believe we lost Mrs. Perkins in the fire." Samuel rubbed her shoulder, trying not to think about the images that were now literally burned into his mind. "She died on her ranch, loving her life." Samuel choked a little on his words of comfort and swallowed hard. "She gave so freely of her time. This community will really miss her and what she brought to it."

Abby looked up at Samuel with tears brimming in her compassionate brown eyes. "Was anything saved from her place?"

"She was such a smart rancher…" Samuel spoke softly, not wanting Abby to know the unwavering ruthlessness of the fire. "When the fire started, she turned her livestock loose and let them fend for themselves. A few smaller animals were found dead. I think her dog Mick was with her. That faithful dog never left her side—even at the end."

Abby took a deep breath, trying unsuccessfully to hold back her tears. Mrs. Perkins had been so helpful with the school. She had loved Abby and her students, and they had returned her love. Abby knew she would always fund a needed item or a project if she were asked. She had provided the means to build the storm shelter and was always there to buy coats for any student who didn't have one or couldn't afford one. Abby sniffled again as she remembered her friend. Samuel patted her shoulder reassuringly, allowing her time to work through her memories and feelings of grief.

"When will we have her services? Have Anna and Parker made any plans?"

Samuel hesitated to answer her questions. *How do I tell her? How do I tell Abby there was no body for burial?* Instead of answering, he changed the subject. "Well, they are waiting on our new wedding plans."

Her head jerked up. "Why? Our plans can be adjusted, but we have to tend to Mrs. Perkins first."

He cleared his throat. "Well," Samuel paused as his emotions came fresh and raw, "we will have a memory meeting for her. We can have it whenever we want."

Abby stared at him, with a slight frown on her face as she let his words soak in, thoroughly, completely. Pressing both lips tightly together, with tears slipping down her cheeks, she gave in her to grief. "Oh, Samuel…" Her shoulders slumped when she finally added, "we have to make it right for her."

"We will, Abby. We will. What do you think about Saturday afternoon when the town is full of folks anyway? After all of this, we need to make it as easy as we can on everyone."

"I know. I know…" she sighed. "The practicality of the West is always rule number one: not always what we want, but what we need." She dried her tears with her hanky. Samuel wiped one away she had missed with his thumb.

"I'm sorry, honey. So, so sorry." He held her close, gently caressing her shoulders.

"How many other buildings in town or other ranchers were lost?" she asked as her head rested once again on his shoulder.

"The Grahams lost everything they had rebuilt from the last fire. I feel so sorry for the old man and Peter. They had really put a lot of work into the place."

"Oh, no." Abby shook her head. She had taught Mr. Graham to read along with the elderly Ranger Tex. They had done quite well and could now read most any story in the newspaper. Peter, his son and a former student, was doing a great job of improving their little farm. "What a loss!" Abby murmured with real empathy for her friends.

Samuel continued, "Quite a few acres burned as the wind took the fire farther East. It kind of skirted around most of the town, even missing the new gambling halls and saloons. The old barracks we cleaned up for the wedding company from Austin was a total loss. Liz and the others had to choose which buildings to save and where to fight the fires. By the way, how is Liz?" he stopped to ask.

"She is totally exhausted. Her dress was ruined, even burned up on one side. Her hands and shoulders are mostly sore from the work of beating the fire and hauling water. One hand did get burned by a hot shovel. We used lavender and tea tree oil mixed together with some bacon fat to rub on them. She said the concoction really helped take away the pain of the burn. You know Liz. Of course, she didn't slow down to get her gloves and never stopped fighting the fire once all night. Her horse brought her home with her slumped over his back, sound asleep."

Samuel chuckled and shook his head as Abby recanted the story. He had to silence his chuckle over the loss of her dress. "Emma, Megan and the girls all seem okay?" he asked, knowing the answer but asking anyway.

"Yes, they stayed at the house with the babies and kept an eye out for the home front."

"I'm so proud of you girls," he stated firmly. "Abby, you hung in there, working against that fire right beside me."

He looked lovingly at the sweet face and curly brown hair of his bride-to-be. "You are a real Texas woman—no Southern belle left in you," he joked.

She smiled at his compliment and teasing. "I'm sorry our wedding plans are all tangled up. What are we to do about our guests and your friends from Austin?" she asked as she twisted on the bench to look straight at her almost husband.

"As long as I get to marry you, the love of my life, I don't really care how much of a to-do it is."

She watched his face anxiously as he spoke, making sure she believed him completely.

"Anyway, Tex is already a day's ride on the road to Austin. He will have enough time to catch them before they leave to come here for the wedding." Tex, who had formerly worked with Sam Houston, was planning to leave after the wedding anyway.

Samuel thought a moment before he continued, "I didn't realize what good friends Tex and Sam Houston were."

Tex had blazed a trail following dusty hoofprints across most of Texas. His weathered face attested to decades of gritty wind and scorching sun. His gait suggested he had been stomped a few times along the way. Among those worn trails of sagebrush and mesquite trees, he had developed a rock-solid reputation as a lawman. He was strong-willed and goal-oriented as he had helped shape the Texas landscape. The love of the land and the pride of his country were very important to Tex. His cunning eyes would gently roll across the pasture or wooded land or ridges or hills where he had fought Indians, outlaws, and wild coyotes. He needed Texas more than the breath that sustained him, and Texas needed him. From the Buffalo Bayou to the Brazos, he knew it all.

"Tex and Sam Houston helped write the history of Texas and could tell firsthand stories of it all. He wasn't one of the chosen families to settle Texas in the 1820s but came during that time as a young man. He has fought Mexicans, Indians and outlaws. He is gonna stay and help preserve some Texas history now that he can read and write. He knows Stephen Austin, Governor Elisha Pease, Lubbock, and all of the men that made Texas what it is. The stories in that one life, I can't begin to imagine!" Samuel sat musing, thinking of the depth of his words.

Abby knew of Governor Pease as well. He was the man who had written the law that established school funds for Texas. She had taught her students about his work with the establishment of railroads, the state penitentiary codes and how he tried to help with the Indians' education.

"Do you think the governor will have any luck convincing any of them to stay with the Union and not secede?" Abby worried over the coming decisions. She had heard more about the controversy than Samuel realized.

"After the John Brown raid last fall on the U.S. arsenal at Harpers Ferry, Virginia, every state in the South is concerned about their rights," Samuel explained.

"I don't understand all of this political nonsense," Abby admitted. "Won't it just all work itself out over time?" Her worry went from the past to the present to the future.

"That 'over time' has been the past sixty years," Samuel stated as he rubbed her cheek. "With the expansion of the West after the war with Mexico and all of the acquired land becoming territories and states, tensions have heated to a slow but steady simmer. They are worried about how the future states will decide the issue of slavery. I'm afraid there is no turning back. This presidential election, I fear, will be the final decision, and maybe even the final straw, for the Southern slave states."

Even though the serving Democratic president, James Buchanan, had been a Southern choice for the current office, the South was discontented with him and his support during his years in office. Now with a new presidential race in place, it looked as if a man named Abraham Lincoln was gaining in popularity for the office. With the Democrat party divided, there wasn't much of a chance for a Presidential win.

Samuel stood and now paced the porch, deep in thought of war, weighing one thought against another. "If Lincoln wins, he will need to gain the support of the North to go into battle. Too many New Yorkers and New Jersey businessmen have their pockets lined by the cotton of the South. They are pro-Southern, and many live in those beautiful homes along the river in Natchez, Mississippi. Many of their children have married into those wealthy, farming families. Blood and money have mixed with emotion at an all-time high. It won't be easy for them to choose. In all truthfulness, I don't see a chance to secede peacefully either."

Chapter 12

The weekend came a few days after the fire. Life had returned to normal, but the sooty blackness of the earth and the battered buildings and ranches still stood as a monument of the event. On the way into town, wagons and ranchers stopped to look at the aftermath of their worst fear and said a quick prayer it wouldn't find them next.

The men seemed to gather on the wooden porch of Samuel's law office. The general consensus was that a spring storm had popped up right at Mrs. Perkins' ranch; lightning had hit her house and the haystack next to the barn. She would have had very little time to respond to the fire, and since she was alone on the place, she didn't stand a chance. As the fire gathered in fury and intensity, Mr. Graham's property was the next barrier in its path. With only him and Peter there, the two had barely enough time to turn their animals loose and get out of the way of the fire. Most of the surviving livestock that had belonged to Mrs. Perkins had been found, gathered and given to Peter Graham and his dad. This "gift" would help them with another new start, which seemed to be the motto of the West.

Starting over was nothing "new" to these homesteaders. No one would let a bad day or a bad harvest stop them. As soon as the setback was over, the people would begin sowing again. The community had decided to honor the memory of Mrs. Perkins by giving her remaining livestock to the Grahams.

Samuel had already posted a letter to her granddaughter, Miss Hanna Deagan, telling her of Mrs. Perkins' passing and asking how she wanted the land and accounts settled. The last he knew, Hanna had been living in Atlanta, Georgia. Hanna's mother was a daughter of the Perkins'; she had married Charles Deagan from Atlanta and had one daughter before she died. Hanna had never met her grandmother, but Mrs. Perkins spoke of her only living relative with great fondness. Samuel was sure she would sell the land and have the money sent back East to her. Mrs. Perkins had already spoken with Samuel about what to do when she passed on through the pearly gates.

Pastor Parker rang the bell at the school, signaling the town that the time had come to gather for Mrs. Perkins' memorial service. Everyone gathered at the cemetery at the end of the main road by the church and school.

Liz stood at her double red doors and watched the migration of people coming out of every business in town. She noticed how full the town was on that Saturday. Wagons had come from far and wide to honor Mrs. Perkins, and truth be known, to see the remains of the fire.

"My goodness," Katie Longmont stated as she stood with Liz and held Iris, her youngest, by the hand. Iris twisted away, wanting to go stand with her friend, Mattie, at the porch post.

Mattie stared at the crowds moving down the street. Since she was at the Mercantile several days a week, she knew most of everything that went on and considered herself an equal of the grown women who were patrons at her mother's shop. "All of these folks are here for Mrs. Perkins," Mattie stated as she put her arm around the shoulder of Iris. "She's gone to heaven in a firestorm—just like Elijah."

Katie and Liz smiled at each other as they watched and listened to the exchange.

"Okay, girls, let's put on our best manners and go tell Mrs. Perkins goodbye."

Jodi Barrows

"But, Momma, why?" Mattie enquired. She turned to her mother with a questioning look. "She's already gone."

Katie covered her mouth to hide her slight giggle, and Liz tried to take Mattie's question seriously and not laugh at the girls. Persistent in wanting an explanation, Mattie continued to look at her mother, who could think of no easy answer, and said, "Remember, Momma? Absent from the body, present with the Lord!"

"Yes, Mattie," her mother stated, "you are correct. It's a matter of going to the church to be respectful to her memory and who she was to us, to the school and to our whole community. She was loved by all because she truly cared and helped everyone she came in contact with."

Mattie smiled as if she were happy that her mother understood. She took Iris' hand and skipped down the steps of the Mercantile.

Katie turned to Liz and commented, "That little Mattie of yours could run for office!"

"Oh, tell me about it," Liz exclaimed as she hitched up Sofie on her hip and turned to lock the door of the Mercantile.

"Sofie doesn't talk much yet, does she?" Katie asked.

"Why would she with her sister managing her life?" Liz replied as she laughed. The women started walking toward the group now gathered at the gravesite. Thomas, Luke, Samuel, Pastor Parker all stood at the cross of her grave. After Luke had given the cross one more thump with his hammer, it stood tall and steady—like the life of the steadfast lady it was memorializing.

After Anna sweetly sang the hymn "Amazing Grace," Pastor Parker cleared his throat and began.

> In Hebrews 4:4, God speaks about a place of rest—good news to our ears and sustenance to our hearts when we grieve over the loss of our friends and families. This place called heaven is only for those who believe in God and what

Jesus did on the cross for us with the sacrifice of His only Son who was sinless. He died that day to wash away our sins so that we could gain entrance to this place God prepared for us long, long ago. God tells us that a rest is good. He made Sunday for rest, for us 'cause He knew we needed it. We are hardworking folks out here and see much work ahead of us and our friends. But we will help one another and rise from these ashes and broken hearts.

Today, you must listen to God's voice and not harden your hearts toward Him for what we have experienced here. For God's Word is full of living power and is sharper than any double-edged sword, cutting deep into our innermost thoughts and desires.

When Pastor Parker finished eulogizing Mrs. Perkins, he read an uplifting Scripture. Then he added, "Thomas is going to start by telling a 'Mrs. Perkins' story, and Luke will conclude. Mrs. Perkins was a person who loved helping wherever she was needed. If you would like to share a thank-you or a word of appreciation for her, feel free to do so now."

"My favorite story is one that Mrs. Perkins told me and a few others present here today." Thomas nodded at a few of his friends.

It was when she was newly settled on her homestead, and she and her family lived in a dugout cabin before her home was built. Not many were around then—pretty much just them and the wilderness of Texas. She said that while she was preparing a meal one day, she heard a thud and felt dust falling on her from the ceiling. She turned to see what had made the thud and spotted a large rattlesnake, lying stretched out, end to end, on her table. She had been using a cleaver in her meal preparation and simply turned and chopped the stunned snake into two pieces. As I sat at her table, she showed me the marks where the cleaver did its work. I told her we could sand down her table and repair it if she liked. She shook her head, said, "No" and added, "It's a daily reminder of the work we have done here and an encouragement for tomorrow if it comes."

The crowd at the graveside smiled and nodded their heads in agreement as Thomas told his story. Much could be learned from the grit and determination of Mrs. Perkins.

The onlookers were quiet for a moment as they all remembered their exchanges with this incredible lady. Then, like popcorn, voices were heard across the crowd that covered the cemetery and road.

"She gave me a chicken."

"She brought me food when I was sick."

"She paid my bill at Liz's store."

"She baked a pie for my birthday."

"She loaded firewood in my wagon last winter."

"She helped me with my laundry when the wind blew it down."

"She brought back my cow when it wandered onto her land."

"She traded eggs with me when she had a hen house full of chickens producing plenty of eggs."

"She cried with me when my baby died."

The crowd looked around at all the voices as her love floated on the air surrounding them all.

After sharing a few more verses of Scripture, Luke concluded the memorial service.

Mrs. Perkins held a special place in all of our lives. She loved the school and provided for many needs over the years. But the one that continues to help us every year is the storm cellar. She paid for the supplies to build the cellar and the large outhouse before school even started the first fall. We will all miss her.

Anna led the townspeople in a song, and the group sang softly in sweet reverence for the lady rancher. Then they gathered to say their goodbyes to a lady who would certainly never be forgotten.

Liz, Abby, Megan, Anna and Katie gathered under the big oak tree between the school and the churchyard. "I hate to ask so soon after the funeral, but are we ready for the wedding in the morning?" Anna asked the group.

"Yes," Abby said sadly. "I wish Mrs. Perkins could be here. She was always the one who organized the community food at get-togethers." She dabbed at her cheeks. "How she loved community gatherings!"

Anna hugged Abby. "She loved you and the school. She will be here in your heart for your celebration."

Emma had been on the edge of the crowd, not too far away from her restaurant during the ceremony. As she walked back, she thought about death and the afterlife. She wasn't sure what she believed. She knew what preachers said from the Bible thumping, but for some reason, the thought didn't settle well with her today. *The old question "If God loved us so much, why would He let us die?" plagued her. Why not let us live on forever—especially the good folks like Mrs. Perkins? She was selfless and always helped others. She seemingly helped everyone in a fifty-mile radius and never boasted of it. She even taught Emma how to manage her chickens. It's hard not to harden your heart, God. Pastor Parker was right to preach on that,* Emma thought. *What he asked us to do wasn't easy. I have much thinking to do on this matter.*

Before she could complete her thoughts, hungry customers had begun lining up at her door, waiting for her to reopen the restaurant. She sighed. *I'll just have to think this through later. Maybe I'll even gather enough courage to talk alone with Heath Parker about it.*

❀ ❀ ❀

Katie and Megan went to the house to put the little ones down for a nap. Lydia was always the easiest. She would smile and roll over with her blanket. Sofie, Iris and Mattie required a little more effort. Mattie poked out her lip at her Aunt Megan. "But I'm not a baby anymore," the almost-four-year-old protested.

"No, you're not. You are almost completely grown," Megan stated as if it were a fact. "But sometimes even grownups need a rest. And Saturday or Sunday is a good time, so just close your eyes for a little while," Megan coaxed. "When you wake up, we will go check on the duck eggs and see if they are any closer to hatching."

That suggestion seemed to help, and the busy, little girl finally closed her eyes.

It didn't take long for the town to settle down. Luke tied Thunder at his mother's hitching post. She glanced out the window by the door and waited for the sound of boots on the wooden steps and the jingle of the mercantile door. He came right in, looking handsome and confident.

Without any hesitation, he pulled her into the circle of his arms and kissed the top of her head. Without releasing her, he started talking. "We don't like goodbyes and long, windy farewells. My horse is packed. I've told Thomas and the men goodbye, the little girls yesterday and the ladies at the house just now. I've saved you for last, Ma." Liz felt the warm burn of her tears sting her face. Her chest quivered in a few breaths as she bit her lip. She didn't look up or release the hug; she couldn't. She let him finish. When they finally looked at each other, she tried to smile but couldn't.

He couldn't quite understand her when she spoke. "I thought you would wait for the wedding tomorrow. Samuel and Abby's." She added the names like he might have forgotten.

"Oh, Ma, you know there will always be one more thing. I'm way behind anyway. I'll have to push hard as it is in order to get to Wyoming."

She nodded because she understood, but she still had no words for her firstborn—only tears—bottled-up tears for Mrs. Perkins, the fire, and now saying goodbye to her only son. "I love you, Luke. I'm so proud of you," she managed to whisper while pulling a hankie from her pocket, wiping her face free of the flow of tears she couldn't have stopped if she had tried.

"Don't cry. Don't worry." He hugged her tightly again, released her, turned and walked to the door, knowing his staying any longer wouldn't help her. Looking back at her, he responded, "Love you too."

She nodded, watched him go and then followed him out the door. Outside, all her friends and family were standing on the street by Thunder, waiting to wave goodbye to Luke. She watched her only son throw his leg over the back of the dark horse as the animal circled in the street. He turned to wave at the crowd, then gently spurred the horse and trotted down the main street toward the edge of town.

Thomas stood with his arm around Liz as they watched Luke and Thunder race out of town, leaving behind a fog of dust and sadness. Liz turned to Thomas and sobbed against his chest.

Chapter 13

Mattie sat on the steps of the Mailly home and watched the baby ducks waddle behind their mother. Her lips were pursed slightly in thought.

"What is it?" Liz asked as she pulled on her white cotton gloves. Her hands were still raw and sore from being burned and fighting the fire from a few days ago.

Mattie looked up in disappointment. "Yesterday, Aunt Megan said, 'Close your eyes, take a nap, and we will watch the baby ducks hatch when you wake up.' When I woke up they had hatched without me!"

Liz now understood. "Oh, honey, I'm sorry. That is just nature. We don't always know when things will happen."

Mattie cocked her head to one side, thinking about what her mom had said. "Nature," she finally repeated, filing the word away in her mind for future use.

"Time to grab your bonnet and head to the church. Today is Abby's and Samuel's wedding."

Megan, Jackson and little Lydia rattled out on the porch with Thomas and the wedding couple. Jackets and string ties on white, freshly pressed shirts were the attire for the men. All of the women and children were dressed in their "Sunday clothes" except for Abby. She carried her wedding dress wrapped in a sheet so as not to soil it or let her groom see it.

The plans were to gather together at the church for the wedding.

Then the preaching with the meal would follow immediately. Ranchers and farmers would need to travel home and put things back in order. As always, the code of the West was necessity—not society.

The church was already packed with many folks who had come to town for Mrs. Perkins' funeral yesterday and the wedding of the town lawyer and the schoolteacher today.

Abby dressed in the school side of the church where both Liz and Megan had prepared for their weddings. She carefully laid her dress on a school desk and unwrapped it from the sheet protecting it. Liz admired the work of art and held the dress open while Abby stepped each petticoated leg into the slim-fitting dress with no bustle. The princess waistline was smooth and fitted in the front with heavy gathers in back, replacing the bustle. The seventy-two crocheted white buttons disappeared down the back into the yards of satin and lace.

Megan stood in awe of the fashionable dress she had sewn. *If only the streets of Paris, France, or even Austin, Texas, could see the dress before her,* she thought.

"It's stunning!" Liz exclaimed. "You look absolutely stunning, Abby!"

Abby was tall and slender. Her dark curls tumbled over one creamy shoulder, and her hair swept up on the other side. Small curls caressed her face where a pearl hair comb pulled her locks up and away.

Emma stared at her sister. "Abby, your hair with Megan's gown is exquisite. The pearl hair comb Samuel gave you is perfect!"

Abby felt beautiful and loved. She gathered her sister and cousins close in a tender hug. "I love you girls—so very much," she whispered. "I never dreamed that life would be this good when I left Mississippi and came West with you."

Liz hugged her cousin a little tighter. "God is good!" She smiled.

"My dress wasn't nearly as hard to get into as we had thought with all the buttons in the back," Abby said as she released her loved ones and stepped back.

"We better get seated, "Megan said quickly.

Anna, seeing the women were ready for the wedding to start, signaled Zeke to begin playing his fiddle. She joined her voice with perfection to the notes and sang as Abby entered the church building. The church was quiet as a real wedding unfolded before them. Abby's wedding was a fairy-tale dream for most of the onlookers as couples generally stood before a judge in common, everyday attire. Some had family attend with a meal afterward, but never anything like this. A beautiful, dark-haired maiden, wearing a handmade gown of imported satin and lace, was marrying the country's "prince" in the middle of the western frontier. Certainly, events like this had to be where folk tales and fables were made!

Daisy, a fourth-year student of Abby's and the oldest of Katie Longmont's children, had handpicked fresh, spring bluebonnets. She had wrapped them in some of the leftover lace from the wedding gown. Before Abby started her walk down the aisle to marry her Samuel, Daisy had handed the vibrant blue bouquet to her teacher. When Megan saw what she had planned, she knew Daisy's idea was a splendid one and congratulated the youth on her thoughtfulness.

Abby's wedding dress was certainly something that belonged in big churches back East and in the highest society circles or the prestigious Southern plantation balls. Here on the edge of civilization and Indian territory, Abby's gown was the most beautiful garment anyone had ever laid eyes upon.

The church was hushed as Anna sang, and Abby walked the short aisle to the front. Samuel couldn't take his eyes off his bride.

He realized he needed to start breathing when Pastor Parker smiled and started to bless their union. Samuel heard nothing as his friend spoke of marriage and read Scriptures from Genesis. Before he knew it, the ceremony was over, and he was listening to some of Abby's students, who were serious as they read a poem for their teacher and her groom.

Abby blinked, and she realized she was now Mrs. Samuel (Abigail) Smith! Cheers and clapping erupted from the crowd sitting and standing in church. She looked at her groom, who was handsome and confident. She could see the love in his eyes as he leaned closer and gently placed a kiss on her lips, completing the beautiful wedding ceremony.

They sat together on the front church bench and listened to the quick sermon. Abby couldn't concentrate on the preaching. She kept looking at her hand in Samuel's. *I'm now a married woman!*

In the style to which Fort Worth was accustomed, delicious dishes of all types were placed on the groaning boards, which served as tables, to serve the food family-style. Thomas, Liz's husband, was asked to pray for the celebration meal. After the prayer, a hearty "Amen" was heard, and the guests lined up in rows on each side of the board table to fill their plates.

Most of the men gathered together to talk about spring crops, ranching, and the devastation from the prairie fire. Several made plans to help the Grahams with raising a cabin and some out buildings. Jackson came up to the group of men, and the conversation turned.

"Jackson?" Mr. Longmont asked, "What do you know of all the tribes being gathered and moved to Indian Territory at the end of last year? Have they all gone?"

After swallowing his bite of chocolate cake, he replied, "I'm not sure." Most of the men had finished eating, but Jackson had been kept busy minding little Lydia while Megan attended to the meal with the rest of the ladies. "All of the tribes are to be in a reserved Indian Territory, but I'm sure several bands haven't complied or haven't heard. It's a large territory to cover for the cavalry, and it's a hard treaty to enforce."

"I was wondering," Mr. DeJarnette, a fellow rancher and good friend of Jackson's, asked, "with Mrs. Perkins gone now and buried here at the church cemetery, where is Mr. Perkins buried? What happened to him? Did anyone ever meet him? As far as I know, they were the first ones to homestead here."

The men looked back and forth at each other, waiting for anyone who knew Mr. Perkins' story to speak up.

"Samuel, how about you? Did she ever say anything to you?"

"No," he replied and looked at Jackson. In his duties as a Ranger, he had been in the area before most of the settlers and homesteaders. Even with everyone waiting for him, Jackson stood silent at first. "Well," he faltered, "Tex told me a story once, and it's a hard one to tell—probably the worst Tex had ever seen. Over 25 years ago, the Perkins were homesteaders here in the middle of nowhere in Indian Territory. Of course, no fort or anything was here, and most people were much farther south. The Perkins had nothing but snakes, coyotes, Indians and buffalo herds for company. There was a settlement about 125 miles south of here. A large Baptist group built a walled fort next to the Navasota River to protect themselves. Anyway, Tex saw smoke trails from a distance and followed them. He came across the Perkins' homestead, and when he came over the ridge, Tex saw a young woman holding a baby that had..." Jackson stopped, swallowed and looked toward Megan and Lydia.

"Go on!" Jeremiah Longmont urged Jackson to continue.

Jackson dropped his head and stared at the floor as he barely whispered, "The baby's head was bashed in."

The shocked men looked in horror at each other.

"Tex rode slowly up to the cabin. Smoke was coming from the remains of the barn. A horse in the corral had been slit open but was still alive. Tex knew the animal had to be put down, so he shot it. And, Mr. Perkins, well, the Indians had done their work well. He had been tied to a fence post, and a wooden stake had been plunged through his chest. They had built a fire under him, and all that was left of him was still burning. A little girl about four had arrows fastening her to the swinging front door of the cabin. Somehow none of the arrows had touched her body, and she was still alive, though in deep shock, and Mrs. Perkins kept clutching the body of the dead baby. Tex didn't know how long she had been there like that, but definitely long enough for the fires to burn down. Her shotgun was lying on the ground beside her. Twenty-one dead warriors and several war ponies were scattered around the grounds."

The men remained silent, shifting from one foot to the other as if they were trying to escape from the thoughts and the brutal picture Jackson had painted for them. They all knew this scenario could be at their home as easily as it had been at the Perkins' ranch that fateful day.

"Tex stayed a while to help her and the little girl. Mrs. Perkins finally decided to send her daughter back to Atlanta to live with her family. She said she could never leave the ranch where her husband and her baby died at the hands of Indians. Neither could she let her older daughter stay and take the chance of her being hurt any further than she already had been.

"Tex always wondered why the Quahadis had never returned to Mrs. Perkins' ranch for all those years to finish what they had started.

Later, he heard a chief talking about the white warrior lady on the Trinity Fork who had fought off his best warriors. They called her 'White Buffalo Heart,' saying she was a great warrior with spirit, and they respected her by leaving her alone in her cabin. She rebuilt her ranch and told Tex that she often saw braves along the edge of her land, but they never bothered her. Several times she would even find a freshly slaughtered deer at her doorstep. Shortly after the raid, she gave birth to a son and raised him at the ranch. He died as a young boy when a tornado went through her ranch. The twister picked him up and tossed him around before dropping him to the ground. She looked for him most part of a day before finding him. Mrs. Perkins and her ranch have certainly seen more than their share of what we battle in Texas.

"Not long after the attack on the Perkins' ranch, nine-year-old Cynthia Ann Parker and her cousin, Rachel Plummer, were stolen by the Comanche at the Parker Fort on the Navasota River."

Everyone stood speechless as Jackson finished his story. Each man was deep in thought, concerned over his own ranch and family. Any given homestead was at the mercy of the weather and a renegade band of Indians. Years had passed since the abduction of the Parker girls, but they had never been found.

After a moment of silence, Jeremiah Longmont turned to Heath Parker. "Are you part of the Parker Fort?"

"Yes," the pastor was quiet and reserved. "My dad was one of the men who escaped. He joined the Army to fight the Indians and look for the girls. That was how I met Anna; her father was the smithy for the Army here in Fort Worth."

Chapter 14

Luke couldn't even remember how many days had passed since this suntanned Texas cowboy had saddled up before daybreak, swung his leg over his old pony, and hit a long lope to where his herd had settled for the night.

"Well, Thunder," he drawled to his horse, who was like his best friend. "It must be good to see the land as God created it. We haven't seen any riders or homesteads for a good long while. I don't know about you, but I could use some sleep in a hayloft and something cooked in a kettle over a stove instead of on a stick over a campfire." He still carried a good supply of jerky and hardtack in his saddlebag, but it didn't mean he looked forward to eating it.

Luke continued north in the known Indian lands across prairie, canyons and rolling hills. Many days held sunshine, but the prairie wind was like a fierce beast he had never before faced. Big rolling weeds tumbled past in droves. Some that were full of prickly thorns or stickers hit him and Thunder. The ones he burned at night put off a good heat but were gone in a matter of moments.

He had only been on the trail a few days when he met a small wagon train comprised of twelve wagons that almost entirely belonged to the same family. The travelers welcomed him around the campfire that night and offered to share their food. He could see the meal bubbling in the pot and the idea of sharing a hot meal with company was appealing. Luke didn't have much to offer back in trade, but they didn't seem to mind much.

Around the campfire that night, they talked of poisoned waterholes, rattlesnakes and the worry of Indians. Luke listened carefully to learn all he could. "So I should look for a pile of animal skulls, a 'P' carved in a nearby tree or even the word spelled out in the rocks…" Luke repeated what the older man had said about poisonous waterholes. "Are there a lot of bad watering holes?" he asked.

"I think mostly as we head on west to California and through the desert. If there's a running creek or river, it should be fine," the trail guide offered. He took a closer look at Luke's spurs. "What's that on your spurs?" He reached around the campfire and spun the silver star spur on the boot Luke had propped up on a barrel.

"I worked at the Rolling M Ranch close to Fort Worth, Texas. That emblem on my spur is the Rolling M cattle brand." Luke glanced at his spur and dropped his foot to the ground. He wasn't sure he liked this guy as well as the old one. *That guide has a look in his eye that bothers me.*

❂ ❂ ❂

As the sun began to set at dusk, a young boy about eleven finished his chores and joined the men and Luke around the campfire. He listened to the men talk, but spoke up when the conversation hit a quiet spot.

"So 'cause of wagon trains like ours going west to California, they want a path cleared for mail and supplies of a sort?" He had overheard Luke talking about his mission and wanted to know something more about what he had heard.

"Yes." Luke smiled at the boy. "In the last ten years, about 300,000 have traveled the two thousand miles across country. Most have gone the Southern route that John Butterfield forged with his stage line. He has a suitable mail route using four-horse coaches, old frontiersmen and the likes. Most of his mail takes at least twenty-five days or longer to reach its destination. The men in Congress think that is best 'cause a northern, slightly shorter route is too risky much of the year due to weather and the Rocky Mountains. Of course, the mail can take months going by ship around the Horn. Lots of cash too." He paused for a moment and then continued. "The other two trails—the Oregon Trail or the Mormon Trail—take almost the same route as the Pony Express' trail. However, they head north when the Pony trail swings down to Sacramento, California."

The old man chuckled. He had a good laugh, making Luke think of his grandfather Lucas. Then the old man started to share his thoughts. "The newspaper said if Hell was in the West, Americans would cross Heaven to get there. I guess they were right. I sold our farm—lock, stock and barrel—in Indiana. Got enough money to come West, but we had to travel on our own because the wagon trains cost $1,200 to join. We then had to put out another $110 for a new overland wagon." He glanced at the wagon beside him, patted the strongly build schooner and added, "That pair of oxen was $60 bucks, and I bought this here guidebook." He pulled the dog-eared manual from his inside coat pocket. "We were gonna go it alone, but we picked up a few other wagons that didn't have the cash to join the big trains either. They made me their wagon master—guess 'cause I have the book."

Luke looked at the front cover and read the title, *Gorms Overland Guide.*

"Plus all of the flour, bacon and coffee cost 15 cents a pound."

"Why did you go?" Luke asked the man straightforward.

"I can get 320 acres, plus my wife can get 320 acres of her own, and if you have a child get married on the trail, the new couple can each get 320 acres. This land is literally a gold mine."

Luke looked over toward the grown daughter, who was sitting

toward the end of the wagon bed. She had been listening but had never joined in. Her hair was held back by her bonnet, so Luke couldn't quite make out the color. He noticed her hair had no curl or bounce in it like his family of women back home. He watched for a moment as she pulled a needle through the hem of a homespun, checked dress. She folded it a good two inches shorter and stitched some more.

"That's Susan," a younger man with a shy smile said.

Luke hadn't been told any names yet. He wondered why he had been told her name since no one else's name seemed to matter.

His voice went low as he leaned over to Luke. "Don't go getting any ideas about her or your own 320 acres, and that shorter hem is for better walkin', that's all."

Luke looked back at the stranger, then back to Susan, and his heart went cold. He was now concerned over the safety of the young woman and what the stranger's intentions were toward her.

Sparks flew from the fire as the white-whiskered man dropped two more branches on the fire. "Susan, honey, will you get us some bread from your momma and some of that sweet, fresh-churned butter?"

"Yes, Daddy." She rose and went to the back of the wagon, returning with two bowls and spoons. She lifted the lid of the pot on the campfire with her apron and filled the bowls with beans and bacon. She handed one to her dad and one to Luke. From the back of the wagon, she brought fresh bread and butter in a tin plate. As she handed it to Luke, she said, "Each morning the milk is put in the churn and hung from the bow of the wagon. As we bounce along during the day, the milk is churned into sweet cream butter."

Luke could now see Susan's face as she had pushed back her bonnet, which had now slipped off and had fallen to rest lightly on her back.

"Well, that's a great way to make butter. I sure do appreciate the meal. I'm sure it's better than what I have in my saddle pack. Thank you. Thank you all." Luke could smell the bean soup and was ready for the meal, but he smiled at his supper company first before lifting his spoon.

The group ate silently. The campfire flickered, and the warmth felt good.

"But now there's going to be a Pony Express route that takes the more dangerous one north." The boy's statement sound more like a question to Luke. The boy added, "It has no freight or passengers, just letters?"

Luke chuckled and tousled the boy's hair. He nodded and placed his empty bowl by the fire. "Yes, three men have worked fast and hard getting the route mapped out from St. Joseph, Missouri, to Sacramento, California, across prairies, rolling hills and high mountains, past buffalo herds and old Indian country. Rain or shine, night or day, the mail will travel by horseback. Forty riders go west and forty go east, jumping from one horse to another and speeding on."

"How long do you ride, and how long can a horse run?" the wagon master asked as he rubbed his white, whiskery chin from the drippings of the bean soup.

"Well, from what I understand, a horse goes hard for ten miles or so, and a rider may go fifty to over one hundred miles, changing to a fresh horse every ten miles at each station house."

The group around the fire listened intently as Luke described his future employment. Susan took Luke's bowl, washed it out and filled it for the young guy at the campfire.

Luke continued, "I should have been there by now, but I got a late start. It's a rough few miles on to the Horseshoe Creek Station they'll be starting any day. I may miss the first pass of mail." He looked a bit worried for a moment. "I can't run Thunder that hard; he's a good-spirited horse and loves a good run, but it's still a good distance away." Luke glanced at the younger man who had been staring at Luke until Susan handed him his supper.

"So why do you go west? Three hundred and twenty acres…and a wife?" Luke couldn't believe he asked the last part. He would have to learn to hold his tongue better or learn how to fight better. He didn't feel like the young man had good intentions, and truth be told, he didn't trust him.

The guy looked up, and his eyes were a color Luke had never seen before.

"People go west for three reasons—money, religion or a fresh start," he stated in a relatively even tone that matched his eyes. "You look smart enough. Figure it out."

Before Luke could answer, the old man added more wood to the fire and stirred it, causing flickers and embers to float and twist about in the prairie breeze. A new smoke cloud started to form as the flames grew, and Luke scooted back. The wagon master spoke, "This guy is a hired wage to help us go west. He gets room and board and a wage. If I were younger, I would head west as a hired wage. Ol' Warren here is the lucky one."

Now knowing the young man's name, Luke looked straight at Warren. "Ya, looks like he's the lucky one all right." Luke hoped that Warren didn't skin them all alive in their sleep.

Luke bedded down next to the wagon train circle that night, hoping that sunrise would break soon, and he could politely ride on to his destination at the station bunkhouse. Before he left the next morning, he left two soft, light-grey rabbit pelts as a thank you for the family who had fed him. *It feels good being with a family again and having a real conversation, but it's time to get going.* He saddled

Thunder and rode on north toward the Pony Express station, telling only the wagon master, "Thank you" and "Goodbye."

Luke watched the landscape around him as a few more days and sunsets passed. He pulled up his coat collar. "Thunder," he said as he pulled one leg over the front of his saddle and hopped down for a quick rest. "I wish I had those two rabbit pelts today to stuff around my collar. We must be getting close 'cause it's getting colder instead of warmer." Luke, ready to spring back into the saddle, looked over his horse's back and saw a rider within hollering distance. The stranger's horse stopped, and the man called out, "Friend or foe?"

Luke had never heard such a greeting. "Friend, I guess, and you?" he called back but waited to mount his horse. He would hate to lose Thunder, but for now, the horse made a good shield if the rider happened to be an outlaw.

"Oh, friend, for sure. I don't got a bad bone in my body," he said as he slid down from his horse. He was now close enough to talk in a normal voice. "Are you headed north?"

The man seems friendly enough, Luke thought, as he came around his horse and extended his hand to the rider. "I'm Luke Bromont. And you?"

"I'm William Campbell."

The rider was younger than Luke was. "You alone, William?"

"Ya, call me Will. The guys at the outfit do." Will rolled up a long whip that had fallen loose from his saddle.

"What outfit would that be?" Luke inquired, wondering if the guy even shaved yet.

"Oh, Mr. Waddell. I knew him first, but he's working with two other men, names of Russell and Majors. They have an outfit called the Overland Trail Express. I just bull-whacked a herd of horses and steers to the Horseshoe Creek Station."

Luke perked up. *Those men were the founders of the Pony Express!* "How far away is it?" he asked, excited.

"You riding that black stallion?" Will asked.

"Yes," Luke said, looking around to see if any other saddled horse had stopped for the conversation taking place under the grove of trees.

"That horse you got should get you there in six or eight days. Are you riding for the Pony Express? The first rider should be leaving St. Joe in about three or four days."

"Yes, I am." Luke was excited to meet someone with news he needed. Now he became interested in Will and what he had to say. "You work for them too? You a rider?"

"Ya, just took the first group of cattle and horses to the station number two at Horseshoe Creek. They had a late snow come through that held me there a day and a half. Guess I needed the rest; I slept it most." He checked the leg of his horse. "Ol' Ragged Jim here has been with me through thick and thin. He can cut those horses and herd cattle as best as any man with a whip. I'm not a pony rider—just a bull-whacker."

After sharing some information with Luke about the road ahead, he swung back up on Ragged Jim and patted his neck. The horse turned to go. Turning sideways in his saddle so his words would drift back to Luke, he added, "You got a good horse. Maybe you'll get to the station in time to catch the first ride west."

Luke quickly mounted, waved goodbye to Will and pushed Thunder to a strong gallop. *Six or eight days away,* he thought. He put his head down and spurred Thunder on down the trail Will had come.

The sun rose and set six more days. The wind whipped around Luke, and white drifts of snow were stacked in the shallows and ridges. Once he stopped to pick up a handful of the icy fluff, having never seen it before to examine it. A gust of wind, like a ghost's calling, came from nowhere, chilling him, brushing the snow from his hand, and circling into nothingness. Another ridge of the rolling prairie was before him. *I can't imagine traveling through any more of this!* He was riding every day, trying to get there and had even begun wondering if he had lost the trail somewhere. Almost at the top of the ridge, he heard a horn blast and then another. Luke thought it sounded as if an elk was bugling, but the sound was too long and different. He urged Thunder to the crest of the hill to check the source of the sound.

He spotted a single rider on the trail in front of him. He watched as the lanky, wind-whipped rider, leaning forward and driving his pony hard, lifted the horn and blew again before letting it fall back to the side of his saddle. "Ya! Ya!" the rider yelled to the horse as he leaned in closer to the horse's neck. He whipped the loose ends of his reins to the left and then to the right over the rump of the chestnut animal. Skirting the rugged edge of the trail, he raced on toward the log cabin that had come into view. Luke watched as a man held the reins of a fresh horse and stood steady. The rider galloped in at full speed, slid off the winded horse, flipped the leather cover with four pockets from his saddle to the freshly saddled horse, securing the opening over the saddle horn, and vaulting onto the waiting horse—all in a blink of an eye! The cowboy reined the horse through the trees to the trail, and before Luke knew it, rider and horse had disappeared at a full gallop around the bend.

Wow! Luke thought. *I've found the Pony Express!*

Chapter 15

Spring 1860

Abby and Samuel sat together in their comfortable home above the law office. They enjoyed the peace and quiet except for Saturdays, when the town was full of families and cowboys. Main Street below was noisy as farmers and ranchers gathered supplies and shared the news of the day, week or month.

A group of cowboys went riding toward the new saloon, past the blacksmith's stables and forge. Samuel opened the door and went down the outside, wooden staircase when the rambunctious riders rode past. *Rowdy cowboys and drifters are becoming a little too frequent,* he thought. Samuel was eager to hire a sheriff or a marshal before things got out of hand. Now that these cowboys had a place to hang out and drink, the law-abiding citizens were becoming concerned.

Samuel really wanted to ask Jackson to take the job, but he knew that, regrettably, the women in Abby's family wouldn't be too happy with his taking the position. He had hoped to wait for Tex to return home but didn't know how long that would be or if Tex had been sent on some other outlaw hunt by Mr. Houston. No matter what, trouble was soon to be on the doorstep of Fort Worth.

Liz had told the new barkeeper that she only carried a supply of alcohol for the normal, medicinal needs of her customers and a good bourbon for the men, but she wouldn't use her freight wagons to haul an endless supply of spirits for his saloon. Needless to say, Mr. Terance Barton with his four-day-old whiskers, ragged jeans and a torn rain slicker was none too happy with her. At least, he had sense enough to hold in his hands the hat with two bullet holes while he spoke to her.

Sooner or later, all of the cowboys waltzed past the red doors of the general store into Emma's Table for a good, hearty meal. Mr. Barton was one of them on this afternoon. The door swung open as the bell jingled. Liz had a moment with no customers and had her back to the storefront. Fully expecting Katie Longmont or one of her other friends or customers, Liz was surprised to turn and see Mr. Barton standing across the counter from her.

"Good afternoon, Mrs. Bratcher." He greeted her by her married name and with the manners of a Southern gentlemen.

"Hello, Mr. Barton," she responded, looking over his new attire, "your establishment must be faring well."

He looked down, realizing to what she was referring. "I was a little road-weary on our first meeting. I apologize, ma'am. I didn't see any need to wear my good clothing on the trail as it also attracts thieves or outlaws."

Liz nodded her head with understanding. "How can I help you today?" she asked, wondering with whom he had spoken to learn her married name.

"I came hoping you would make a business deal with me," Barton answered as he smiled with his gleaming, straight teeth shining through his full lips. He held his hat steady in his hands.

For a brief moment, Liz was taken with his good looks and manners. Then she realized she was the mouse and he the cat, hoping to pounce! "Mr. Barton, " Liz replied with firmness, "I will not change my mind on freighting in excess spirits for your establishment. The money I would make is of no consideration to me." She picked up her ledger, signaling she was finished with their conversation.

Mr. Barton didn't back away to leave but stepped to the left in front of her again. "Even if partial monies were given to a charity of your choice?"

She looked up at him again, not taking her eyes from him, "Washing dirty money doesn't make it clean." She paused but kept her eyes fastened on his.

"I see," Mr. Barton said, continuing to fasten his gaze on her. He waited a moment, letting her words linger in the air. He wasn't used to people not bending to his way, and this blonde storekeeper was standing her ground.

"I'm glad you do. Good day, Mr. Barton, "Liz dismissed him politely. He walked all too cavalierly to the door, not showing any signs of anger. As he turned to leave, Mr. Barton caught her eye and with a nod of his head stepped out the door. Liz watched as he went a few steps on the walk and went next door to Emma's Table.

❊ ❊ ❊

Abby put aside her handwork, deciding the time had come to read her mother's letter. It had arrived with her wedding quilt along with the tablets and pencils for her students. She had been hesitant to open it as she was exceedingly happy and didn't want that happiness marred by what her parents would say. She and Emma had both left home without their parents' blessings. Her father was angry, and her mother despaired. Both had tried to control their daughters, but to no avail. The two sisters did not want to displease or anger them, but the box in which they had been kept was too small, the molding too tight, and the love was dependent and controlling.

Holding the unopened letter, Abby paced the small, upstairs parlor. She tapped it in her palm. *What if Mother wrote to make up with us, telling us how much they loved and missed us? Time to find out...*

Abby sat down and inserted the letter opener into the edge of the envelope and quickly slit across the top. She slipped the pages from the envelope and hesitantly opened them to read her mother's words. Only one other letter had come in four years, begging them to come home and then her imploring tone had been followed with a demand to return "this instance!" Abby had written several times a year, but Emma refused to write. Abby sat up straight, preparing herself for the worse and started to read.

> *My dearest Abigail,*
>
> *I trust you and Emma are well, and excitement is high as your wedding day approaches. Your father and I take great joy in your choice for a suitable husband. A lawyer and friend of your governor of Texas is quite a step up in society. I would have chosen to have the wedding in Austin rather than in the tumbleweed town of Fort Worth.*

Abby sighed as she placed the letter in her lap for a moment. Mother must be feeling better, she thought as she continued to read.

> *I assume that it is difficult to make the journey to Austin as receiving letters and parcels via stagecoach is new to your community. At least it is available now to carry our love and well wishes your way. Maybe in our lifetime the railway will allow us the speed of travel, and we can come see your Samuel and your beloved Texas that you and Emma speak of. As uncivilized as it is, I can see that the love of Texas is strong among its people.*
>
> *I don't understand it, but even Mississippi has lost many of its families and men to your great state of Texas and the ways of the West.*
>
> *Your father and I are well, even though the threat of seceding runs high in these volatile, political times. At all of our entertaining, the men are soon shut behind doors with their*

bourbon and talk of war. I so wish it would hurry and happen so we can put those Yankees in their place and get on with our ways.

I do pray that Emma is well and not the dark, sulky youth as I last knew her to be. Your father never speaks of her; it's as if she is dead or never born. I am saddened by our parting. I simply cannot imagine her cooking everyday as our Jasmine does. Such hot, hard work that is never-ending—and managing a chicken farm!? I never would wish that on the most envy-hearted or fault-finding woman I know! Surely, Emma isn't waking to this each morning and not wishing she was back home on the plantation with her father. Manual labor for one of my daughters is unbelievable. Why, we have bought labor for those everyday chores!

Abby dropped the letter to her lap and tried to calm herself. *Why does she even bother to write?* **Our parents are not even trying to understand Emma or me.** *We were only showpieces to them—not suitable heirs—just to be used a dowry for a business deal or to further their rank in society!* Her mother's letter continued in the same tone.

Our crops and plantation are doing well your father tells me. I asked for the carriage one sunny day and took a look for myself as it had been a while since I have ventured into the roads of the field. As you know, I never took a liking to any of this.

I would be remiss if I didn't offer you some womanly advice on the eve of your wedding. Always look your best and attend to your hair and dress. Never let him see you in disarray or a state of confusion. Never worry him on how you would act or represent him or his business. Remember his success is Austin politics or business is dependent on how his wife would *represent him in society. Never voice disrespect to him or embarrass him. Build him up in all the ways that you can. Never confide your worries to another woman. Even if Samuel takes a mistress or a night away from home, look the other way. Never voice your thoughts to him or ask needless questions.*

I do hope you aren't continuing your schoolteacher responsibilities now that you are to marry. For a wife to work and not attend to the needs of her husband doesn't look good.

Abby stuffed the pages into the envelope as she couldn't possibly read one more word. *Why would I want to—except to become even more upset? I'm so glad that Emma and I escaped when we did!*

Abby walked to the window and looked out on the bustling street below. She realized she had become so upset that she had blocked out the noise of the afternoon. Liz's store was bursting with women and their children. Some were even playing on the walk in front of the store. Buggies and wagons were rowed up next to saddled horses at the post. No matter how noisy or busy this town became, this was her town, and she loved it! *I never wanted to return to my former Mississippi home again.*

Abby threw her wrap around her and hurried down the steps. She waved and smiled as she passed Samuel, Thomas, Parker, Jeremiah, and Jackson standing on the walk with a few other men, waiting on their wives to come out of Liz's Mercantile.

As Abby crossed the street and bounced up the steps to the double red doors, she saw that the street all the way to the livery was full of wagons. The store was as busy as the street. Little Dove cut fabric for Katie Longmont. Megan held Lydia while she visited with a new lady Abby had never seen. Anna played with Hope Rose and Katie's littlest girl Iris. Mattie had Sofie by the hand, leading her to where the other little girls were. Abby made her way to Liz at the register where she was assisting another unfamiliar lady with a sale.

"Hi, Abby!" Liz smiled.

"Thank you and come any time," Liz said to her customer.

Abby circled behind the counter, still enraged with pent-up frustration from her mother's words.

Liz recognized the look and asked with her eyes, "What is it?"

"My mother!" exclaimed Abby quietly through clenched teeth.

"Your mother?" Liz asked. "What happened?"

"Her letter…" Abby sighed.

"Her letter? You mean you are just now reading the one that came weeks ago with the quilt?"

"Yes," Abby said, holding her forehead in frustration. "I wish she could write a sweet letter or not write at all. Even with all of these miles and days between us, she's still trying to control us. Now, more than ever, I am so glad we ran away. Father has disowned us, considers us dead. He never speaks or asks or even wonders about his two daughters. It's as if we never existed to him, and Mother never fought for us—just lives in her silly, society walls of false reality and a fake, loveless marriage."

"I'm so sorry, Abby," Liz responded, wishing she had exactly the right words to comfort her cousin.

"You should hear what she told me of marriage. Every word of advice was so controlling and contriving. I would never, never treat Samuel that way, and I don't see you or Anna or Megan having a relationship like that either."

Liz felt sorry for Abby. *She's obviously very upset by her mother's letter. Life is strange,* Liz thought. *Here Abby has a mother who isn't loving, and I had a loving mother who died so long ago. Even though the two women were sisters, they couldn't have been more different.* Liz had always assumed that Abby's father was the one who had done the most damage to the women in the family.

Liz looked Abby in the eyes and tried to think of something to calm her and make her feel better. "Abby, you have a happy life here with Samuel. Try not to let your mother drag you into the past. What you don't see with your eyes, don't invent with your heart. Live for today and look forward to tomorrow. Do you remember what Jesus said about times like this? '...*Don't worry about tomorrow, for tomorrow will bring its own worries. Today's trouble is enough for today.*'"[1]

Abby nodded, knowing Liz was right. A calm assurance began its gentle work in her heart.

Katie called Abby's name and motioned for her to come. Abby patted Liz on the shoulder to say goodbye. Liz nodded and smiled, already helping another customer.

"We need a quilting," Katie sighed. "Do you think you can put one together soon?"

"Yes!" Abby agreed. "Do you know anyone who has a quilt ready to go into the frame?

"I'm sure there are several. I'll ask around—and you too." Katie looked for Iris and tucked her package of new fabric under her arm. Iris fussed a little about having to leave her friends until Mattie cupped her hand to whisper something in the little girl's ear. Iris smiled and waved goodbye until the next time.

Katie wondered what the wise Mattie was up to as she laughed to herself. Spotting Jeremiah as she looked out the door, Katie nodded to him. She located her wagon in the crowd of buckboards and gathered her children to load up. They were a distance from town, and the sunset was always wearing upon them. She and Jeremiah both wanted to be home before nightfall.

Samuel noticed a neatly dressed black man on the street in front of Emma's. He wasn't dressed in Sunday attire, but his clothes were clean and without holes or much wear. The man walked out the door, obviously having enjoyed a good meal and looked up and down the street. Samuel knew of a gathering of free men in Texas. Some could read and write or even possessed skilled labor abilities. This man of average height must have been one of them. He seemingly traveled alone as no other was about. Samuel watched him until the man's eyes caught his. Samuel briefly nodded his head. Then the man glanced in both directions of the street and crossed over to where Samuel stood with the other men.

The newcomer cleared his throat to speak but didn't step upon the walk with the other men. "Would any of you be Samuel Smith or know where I could speak with him?"

"I'm Mr. Smith. How can I help you?"

The stranger looked at Samuel and at the words painted on the window behind him—*Samuel Smith, Attorney at Law.* "Sir, I was told to find you and ask about work at the blacksmith and livery. My name is Luther Wheeler."

"Hello, Mr. Wheeler," Samuel addressed the man. "Come on up on the boardwalk. I'd like for you to meet my friend, Thomas Bratcher, a rancher and the husband of Elizabeth at the general store."

Wheeler nodded his head and looked over to the Mercantile, letting it all sink it. "Also, Jeremiah Longmont, a fellow rancher, and his family is over there waiting in the wagon, Pastor Parker and Jackson."

Wheeler stepped up on the boardwalk, smiling as he met all of the men. "Nice to meet ya'll." He reached into a chest pocket and pulled out some papers. "I suspect you will be asking about my papers. I'm a free man and looking for work. Was told in Birdville by the marshal that Fort Worth was in need of a blacksmith and liveryman. Those are my skills, and I would sure appreciate the chance to prove my work to you."

Jackson spoke first, "Colt—Marshal Colt, how was my friend?" Jackson smiled, remembering his partner. "Rode Ranger with him for years 'til they took rangering away from us."

"Marshal was fine as a frog's hair, sir, and said for me to meet up with you too." Wheeler had a strong Southern accent.

Samuel looked over Wheeler's papers, showing he had his freedom. He wasn't much to the liking of holding slaves and had no problem with a man of color working hard for his livelihood.

"Mr. Luther, I would be happy to give you a run at the livery and ironwork. It belonged to my dad, and the town is sure in need of that help. Any of these men here on the walk are your friends, and you can turn to us any time. I see you had a taste at Emma's. She's my wife's sister and can sure cook a fine meal. You won't have any problem at her place either."

Wheeler was a bit surprised to be met with such friendly talk. He knew his place as a free man of color and wouldn't overstep his place or take advantage of it either. He knew far too well that not all white people would accord him the respect he had received today. Even when a person wasn't looking for trouble, it could easily find him.

"Yes, she cooks a fine meal. I found a table in the back, and she said I was welcome to use the front door. I thank you all for your kindness." He nodded and almost bowed to them.

"Nice to meet you, Mr. Wheeler," Jeremiah said as he started toward his waiting wagon full of family and supplies. "I'll bring some work for you next time I'm in town. I, for one, am happy to have a smithy again." He stepped down from the boardwalk and leaped into his buckboard.

"Let's go look it over, Mr. Wheeler, and see what you think," Samuel said.

"Oh, I know I'm gonna like it all. Thank you, Mr. Smith. I'm gonna like it a lot." He smiled and twisted the soft felt hat he held in his hands.

They walked together up the street to the top of the hill where the livery and shop stood. Samuel showed him the shop, the tools, the stable, and where his dad had lived. Wheeler was more than excited with what he saw. *This is so much more than I expected,* he exulted.

"Shouldn't take too long until we get the business up and rolling again; it's been a while since we have had it working. My father's death was quite unexpected. I feel relatively sure there's a backlog of work just waiting for word that the place is open again. I'll pay you a dollar a week. You can board here, and I'll open a tab for you at Emma's. In thirty days, we will revisit our deal and go from there."

Samuel paused to gaze down on his town as he stood at the front of the building. Some wild cowboys were whooping it up in the newest addition to the town. He noticed that the saloon was the nicest building on the street; it hadn't been touched by the prairie fire. *Mr. Barton and some cowboys must have fought it off,* Samuel thought as he looked over that side of town. Some shanties had popped up since Samuel had been that way. He hadn't ridden down that far the few weeks since he had married. He now realized a mistake had been made and worried over the need for a marshal even more.

Wheeler watched Samuel's face and then noted what Samuel was watching as a frown started to crease his forehead. "Not sure anything good is down there for any of us, Luther."

Wheeler nodded. He removed his pack from his horse that was already tethered at the stable and started to make himself at home. "Thank you, sir," he stopped to say to Samuel.

Threads of Courage

Samuel shook Luther's hand and headed toward his office, stopping once to look back at the end of town that seemed to have grown overnight. He noticed Thomas and Jackson were still standing in front of the law offices. As Samuel stepped up from the street, the two noticed his worried look.

"Everything okay?" Thomas asked. "Luther gonna work out?"

"Have you seen or been down the hill from the livery?" Samuel rubbed his chin.

"Shanties and shacks have popped up since the prairie fire a few weeks ago. I've been so preoccupied with the marriage and Abby and the political scene, I've missed what was going on."

Both men looked the direction of the livery.

"Thomas, Jackson, I'm not so sure a marshal is gonna come our way as easily as our Mr. Wheeler did," Samuel continued with concern. "We sure are in need of one," he paused, "like—yesterday!"

Samuel and Thomas both looked at Jackson.

Jackson looked down and then over to the hill that went down to the saloon and back to his friends. Without saying a word on the topic, he said, "Good day, gentlemen," and stepped down from the boardwalk in one hop as he headed purposefully down the street in the opposite direction of the saloon. They watched him disappear around Emma's building to his weekend home with Megan and Lydia.

---

[1]Matthew 6:34, Holy Bible, New Living Translation, copyright © 1996, 2004, 2015 by Tyndale House Foundation. Used by permission of Tyndale House Publishers Inc., Carol Stream, Illinois 60188. All rights reserved.

Chapter 16

Emma woke up early; in fact, she had tossed all night as she had for the past several nights. She rolled over, folded the quilt down to her waist and sighed as she looked out the dark window. *Might as well get up,* she thought and threw back the covers to free her legs. Emma sat up and ran her hands through her dark curls, then rubbed her green eyes. *Maybe...* she thought as she looked at the empty side of the bed where her sister Abby had slept for years. *Yes, it's 'cause my sleeping partner is gone.* With Abby married, Emma wasn't sleeping well. *I'm sleeping in a half-empty bed.*

"That's it," she stood and said it out loud, happy with figuring out the why of her insomnia. "It must be...and so simple."

Emma quietly dressed, mostly in the dark, then turned up the wick of the lamp to provide more light. She stopped to admire her simple quilt of brown and beige strips, sewn around black and red center squares.

Emma's hands ran across the quilt, smoothing the wrinkles as she pulled up the quilt to make her bed. This quilt was the latest in her collection of handmade quilts. This one had been easy to create as most of her quilts were. Just a row of solid-colored fabric sewn on all four sides of a square. She repeated the color of the center square for the second row of strips then the row of solid color, finishing with the color of the center for the last row of strips. She found finishing the piecing and quilting during the winter months almost effortless and manageable. She had stitched the double-folded binding a few days ago and had hoped the new quilt would help her sleepless nights.

Abby had taken the quilt she and Emma had shared to her new home above the law office. Her desire to take the quilt made Emma happy, knowing her family was very near and shared their love through quilts. This new quilt would take the place of that cherished one they had shared.

As she walked past the bedroom door of Jackson, Megan and Lydia, she tiptoed so the heels of her black boots wouldn't click on the wooden floors and wake them. They still had plenty of time to sleep before sunrise and her rooster crowed his wakeup call.

Since it was still dark, she decided to keep the house quiet and go on to work and start baking. Emma slipped out the front door and strolled along the narrow path that had been worn over the years to her place. Walking in the back door of Emma's Table, she tied her apron in the back and then woke up the low glow of embers in her stove.

"Little Dove, you sweet girl," Emma said to herself as she looked at her water supply. Her helper had filled the buckets before she had left last night. Even though she had a pump at the house, it was surely nice to have the water indoors and not have to go out in the dark again. She added more wood to the stove as it came to life with heat. She scooted her water kettle over the highest red flames.

Never let the fire go completely out, she recalled. Even when she was a young girl, her mother's black cook Jasmine at the Mississippi plantation taught her the finer points of running a kitchen.

Cinnamon rolls were now ready to roll up and slice for the pan. Her thoughts had already traveled in several directions that morning. She was very cognizant of the fact that Liz, Megan and Abby were all married, and she was the only one who slept alone. *Maybe I am subconsciously bothered by that aspect. NO!* She shook her head and vigorously dusted the cinnamon from her hands. "No, not marriage!" she repeated.

Adding more wood to her stove, Emma heard the front door jingle and saw Pastor Parker step in very quietly. "Good morning," he called. "Do you have a coffeepot on yet?"

"No, but it will only take a moment. I have it ready to go on next." She popped in the cinnamon rolls to bake, closed the door of the oven and slid the coffeepot on the flame where her teakettle had been.

"Please, take a chair," she coaxed her friend as she walked over to sit for a minute herself with a fresh cup of hot tea. "My house was too quiet to start the kitchen. So I came over early to bake some breakfast breads."

The chair grated on the wooden floor as she pulled it away from the table where Pastor Parker sat. She looked at her friend, "What're you doing up so early?"

"Sometimes I get up early and walk the streets of the town, praying for all that crosses my mind. The families of each business I pass—people on the street I have visited with or met that week. There is much to pray for." He placed his elbows on the table, folded his hands together and smiled, looking at Emma.

Pastor had a look that suggested he knew what she needed prayer for. She didn't feel uncomfortable but loved. She had never thought of his doing that—praying for the town and all the people he met.

"Hope you don't mind me stopping in this early," Parker said after a few moments of silence.

The coffeepot started to whistle, and Emma slowly pushed out her chair to get him a cup. While pouring the steamy, black liquid in the mug but not looking at Pastor Parker, Emma asked, "How do you know who God is?" As she set the mug in front of him, she looked intently at him. "Megan is sure of Him, and Liz even hears His voice, but…I don't know. If God is so loving and good, why did

Mrs. Perkins die? Why did the fire come and wipe out the Grahams for a second time? Why was our grandfather shot and killed?" As she returned to her seat in front of the pastor, her green eyes begged for an answer to the question that was as old as the stories in the Bible.

Pastor swallowed a sip of hot coffee, undisturbed by her questions. "I think it takes more faith not to believe than it does to believe. I look at the creation of trees and animals and a beautiful sunrise, and I can't help but praise God for His work. Who told the sun to come up? Who put the seasons in place?"

She rested her chin in the palm of her hand and listened as he continued. This time when she had asked, she had really wanted to know. She wasn't trying to be sassy or disrespectful. And she wasn't simply making up hard questions she thought no one knew how to answer.

"Then I ask myself if God is real and He made all of this and put it in a Book so I could know about Him, what does He want? How am I to respond to what He has given us?"

Emma was letting his words soak in. Parker didn't shove religion at her but asked a few questions to which she also wanted to know the answers. After a few moments she asked, "So what did you find out?"

"I went looking in the Bible to see what it said about who God is and what He wanted."

Emma blinked, waiting.

"I found verse after verse all through the Old Testament where He says, 'I am yours, and you are Mine. I will be your God, and you will be My people.' God wants a relationship with us, and He wants us to have a relationship with Him. He made the world as a gift to us with all that we need and can enjoy. God told generation after generation that this is what He wanted. Emma, He wants you. God loves you."

Emma blinked again to clear her emerald eyes. She didn't have an earthly father who loved her and cared for her. It was always 'you do this, and I will love you.'

Even Pastor expressed love by walking the streets of Fort Worth, praying for people—some he knew, others he didn't. The idea of having someone to love her for simply being herself was all new to her. Emma didn't know how to believe or receive God's love.

"Okay," she said, trying to understand. "God wants a relationship with us, and He loves us and gives us what we need."

Pastor nodded in agreement, encouraging her to continue.

"Mrs. Perkins was a good person and helped our town. I think she believed. Why did the fire happen to her and the Grahams? Why do we have hurts and hardships if He loves us so?"

"Remember first that it's about having a relationship with Him. It's important to be good like Mrs. Perkins, but being good doesn't get you to heaven. It's knowing Him. The 'being good' and 'obeying God's Word' will come later as you want to please Him. But we have no control over the bad things that happen," his words trailed off. "Earth isn't heaven, a perfect place. Satan rebelled against God's authority, saying he wanted to be worshipped, held high and praised as God. In Genesis 1:2, God said the earth was dark, chaotic and empty. I think that's when Satan fell from heaven, taking his one-third of the angels he had charge over. Then in verse three, God brought light and form and structure, day and night. Animals and trees and a garden followed. Lastly, God reached down and took some dirt, formed a man, blew breath into him and named that man Adam.

Emma had never heard Scripture make sense like it did now. Pastor Parker had put it together in a story she finally understood.

"You can always go deeper and say God knew Satan would fall. Why would God make him, or why did God allow Satan in the garden with His new creation—Adam and Eve?

Emma nodded, waiting for the answer.

"It comes back to God's allowing you to choose to love Him. Think of it as a parent. Every parent knows his child can have problems or disobey, even rebel in the worst way. But they have chosen to marry and have a child they will love. They try their best in hopes that their child will love them back. It's a willing choice to have a relationship."

The wonderful aroma of baked cinnamon rolls permeated the dining room. Emma jumped up to pull them from the oven just in time. "Would you like one?" she asked as she set them on the stove.

"I surely would!" he exclaimed. He had inwardly hoped they would be done before he moved on for the day!

She removed a big roll from the pan and placed the plate of sticky bread in front of him. Emma tossed over her shoulder the warm towel she had used to retrieve the pan of rolls.

"Thank you, Emma. It looks perfect." He picked up the fork to cut a large piece off from the rest of the roll. The pecans from the family orchard were sticky and seasoned with the cinnamon, butter and sugar mixture covering the bread. He knew Emma was the best cook around and couldn't wait for the first bite to melt in his mouth. Emma went to get the coffeepot to warm his cup.

"Think about what we talked about, Emma. If you have more questions, let me know. But…" he stopped for a moment, "let God talk to your heart and help it make sense."

She nodded her head, "Yes, I will. Thank you, Pastor Parker." She did feel God's love as she had listened this morning. She did believe in God, but she had so many other concerns she seemed unable to line up in her mind.

Chapter 17

Early that morning at the ranch, Mattie and Sofie woke up and ran to their mother's room. "Where is Callie, Momma? Where is she?"

Waking up to their cries of distress, Liz was confused. Usually the cats were put in the barn at night for safekeeping. She glanced toward the window and noticed it was still very dark outside. "Okay, okay," she said, sitting up. "What's the matter?"

"Papa is up and went to the barn, and Princess and her kittens are inside, but Callie is gone. Mama, she's gone!" Mattie wailed. Sofie popped her thumb into her mouth and snuggled closer to her mother's side, blinking to remove the sleep from her eyes.

"Was she put in the barn last night?" Liz asked. She didn't understand why her girls had awakened her and now were so scared and worried over the cats in the barn.

"I think so," Mattie pranced barefoot at the edge of her mother's bed. "Momma, hurry! We have to get her."

Liz pulled on her wrapper and tied it, slipping on a soft pair of slippers. She sat Sofie on the floor. Mattie was twisting at the doorway. "Come on," she urged.

Small streaks of pinkish sunlight were starting to make their way through the windows. Just as the three made it to the bottom of the stairs, they heard the most horrific noise. A cat was yowling and hissing, and *something* else was growling and yapping.

Mattie screamed, "Momma, it's Callie! She needs help!"

"Don't open that door," Liz ordered. She looked for Thomas or Lulu or the gun. All they could hear was more fighting and rolling and bumping about.

Mattie's eyes were getting larger as the noise was getting louder. She placed her hand on the doorknob, "Momma, oh, Momma!"

Liz looked out the window and saw Callie being rolled by a coyote and then tossed to another. She fought, hissed and clawed—only to be surrounded by the three wild animals between the porch on the house and the barn. If the cat ran, they would chase and grab her by the neck again. If she stayed, they had her too.

Liz was afraid the girls would see the cat torn apart or bitten by a wild animal. A little more light pierced the darkness. With all this noise, she wondered where the rest of the ranch hands were. *Surely, they were all up by now.* She grabbed her gun and pulled Mattie away from the door.

"Stay inside," she ordered and opened the door.

Her appearance gave Callie the moment she needed. She took to a fence post, the closest thing to climb. The coyotes turned and took off after her, jumping and charging at the cat on top of the post that wasn't really tall enough to offer complete refuge.

Liz looked back at the porch, making sure the two girls obeyed, and cocked her gun to fire. Frantic, she looked about but in the darkness couldn't see anyone else. She fired, and one coyote slumped to the ground.

Mattie screamed like Liz had never heard her before. She turned to see Sofie pinned at the barn door by a fourth coyote. Her face was white, and though she tried, not a word came from her mouth. Her soft baby checks were face-to-face with his snarling fangs. The other two were still at the post with the Callie, determined to finish their fight.

Liz whirled to the scene at the barn door with her baby. She fired her Colt again, and the animal yipped and stumbled only to stand again. He snarled and growled at Sofie then turned toward Liz as she advanced toward them.

"Sofie, don't move," she yelled. "Mattie, don't move!"

Mattie stood frozen on the porch step. With her fingertips in her mouth, she was frightened by what was happening before her. Her blue eyes darted back and forth between her momma and little sister. Liz fired again, and two more shots echoed hers from somewhere. The coyote in front of her fell, and the growling and snapping behind her also stopped. She turned to see that Thomas had backed her up and shot the two attacking Callie at the post.

Liz ran to Sofie, stepping over the fallen animal to reach her frightened daughter. She had shot the coyote only inches from the traumatized girl. "My poor baby," Liz cried. Sofie clung tightly to Liz and buried her face in her neck and hair. "It's okay. I've got you," Liz soothed as she stroked her hair.

Mattie ran into her father's arms. "Callie, Daddy! We have to help Callie." Thomas scooped her up and turned to the post where the fight was finished. Callie was lying on the ground at the foot of the post. Thomas saw that her fur had been ripped away at her neck, and her ear was hanging loose. The cat wasn't moving.

"Oh, Mattie, honey…I don't know if Callie made it." He stepped closer as Mattie turned to look.

"She has to, Daddy. She does. I know it!"

As Thomas came closer, the cat moved her head ever so slightly.

Liz carried Sofie to the post to watch Thomas and Mattie. Only then did Sofie lift her head from Liz's shoulder to see their cat.

Lulu came around from the kitchen door with a box stuffed with an old cloth for bedding. She knelt down by the cat and carefully lifted her into it before slowly and cautiously examining her.

"No promises," she said as she looked at the two little girls. "But I try to make her better." Lulu picked up the box with Callie and headed to her cabin. Mattie was quiet as she listened to Lulu talk to the beloved cat. She tearfully watched Lulu carry the box with Callie into her cabin.

Thomas looked at Liz, "What happened?"

Liz blinked. "I'm not sure," as she looked at the dead coyotes scattered about the property. "It was dark, and Mattie came to my bed, worried about Callie. When did you get up and leave?" she asked, trying to put the pieces together.

"Couple of hours ago," he answered. "I got up to check on a mare ready to drop, and we didn't have her in the barn. She was so wild, we couldn't get her in the barn in time, so we were tending to her in the pasture. When I heard the commotion and the first shot, I headed back to the house. With the sun not up yet, I couldn't make out who was outside and all that was happening. As soon as I could, I shot the two at the post," he paused to look at the girls. "What are you two doing up anyway?"

When neither of them answered, Thomas asked, "Mattie?" as he turned to his oldest. "When did you get up, and how did you know Callie needed help?"

"I heard you, Papa," she looked sad and now had one finger in her mouth. With a worried look, she glanced at her parents.

"Then what did you do?" Liz asked.

"I went to the window in my room upstairs and saw you leave." She looked at her father. "The barn door was open, and I saw Callie in the light of the door. I tried to go back to sleep, but I heard the coyotes call and yap. Lulu told me that was a hunting yap. I ran to Momma's room to get help." Mattie started to cry.

"How did Sofie wake up?" Liz asked.

"I woke her," Mattie sobbed.

"Let's get dressed. We can talk about this more at breakfast." The girls were quiet as Liz pulled their dresses over each girl's head and fastened the buttons along the back. They all went downstairs where Liz started breakfast since she didn't know when Lulu would return. Thomas came in the back door to a quiet kitchen. He poured a cup of coffee and looked at the tear-stained faces of his girls. "Liz, looks like one of those coyotes might have rabies."

Liz stopped as terror gripped one. "Which one?" she managed to choke out.

"The one that cornered Sofie at the barn."

"Oh, thank You, God!" Liz breathed. "It didn't touch her."

Thomas looked at Liz. "Even if Lulu nurses that cat to life," he paused, "we might have to put her down. Can't take any chances, you know."

"Oh, no, Thomas!" Even as Liz felt heartsick, she realized the danger Callie would present if indeed the cat contracted rabies from the coyotes' attack.

"I won't even pelt the animals. I started a burn," added Thomas, still standing with his cup of coffee as he leaned against the cupboard.

Liz's shoulders drooped as she gazed sadly at her two little girls, eating their pancakes. She sighed. *Seems most certain that Callie won't be around long.*

Chapter 18

APRIL 1860

Jeremiah Longmont drove his wagon load of family members into town early that morning. Stopping at the school first, he helped his daughters, Daisy and Lillie, down from the wagon. Daniel jumped down from the back and sprinted up the schoolhouse steps.

Abby opened the door to let Daniel in and called out to Katie Longmont, "I'll see you later this afternoon."

Holding Iris, Katie waved as she smiled excitedly. "We will leave plenty of quilting for you. Come as quickly as you can."

With a snap of the reins, Jeremiah urged his horses to move on. He turned the wagon and headed to the front door of Liz's Mercantile. Jeremiah helped Katie and Iris safely down from the wagon.

"I'll be at Samuel's for a short while, then I'll be back late afternoon." He kissed Katie then Iris on the cheek and bounded with long strides across the street and up the stairs to Samuel's law office.

Samuel sat at his desk, waiting, and holding a letter.

"Good morning," an out-of-breath Jeremiah greeted Samuel. He shut the door behind him and didn't wait for Samuel to reply. Every man in the whole country was waiting for news about the political parties convening. The Democrats had been first with an April date for their convention in Charleston, South Carolina.

"Good morning, Jeremiah." Samuel swallowed a gulp of coffee. "The first platform placed for a vote was pro-slavery. It was rejected, and delegates from eight states walked out, forcing an adjournment. They couldn't agree on a presidential candidate for the party.

"So we wait again?" Jeremiah asked, trying to understand.

"Yes, the Republicans hold their convention in Chicago next month." Samuel's brow wrinkled with concern. "I'm sure the candidate will be Lincoln as he is already making visits to the Southern states. He talks against separation and pleads with the leaders for a compromise."

"Lincoln sounds like a good man." Jeremiah looked for something good to hang onto. "Why can't our President do anything about this now?"

"Both Houses are working on proposals, but President Buchannan has done little, which has only fanned the flames. His cabinet is furious with him; he is lame now."

Jeremiah listened. "So this Lincoln sounds like he is trying."

"Yes, he's cautious concerning the slavery issues, but insistent that slavery cannot be expanded into the new territories."

"Well, that idea sounds good to me. Why can't the pro-slavery Southern states go with that?" Jeremiah thought Mr. Lincoln's plan sounded both feasible and workable.

"We can always hope, Jeremiah." Samuel didn't think things would end well. He knew too many proud hotheads. With each state having voting rights, the slavery issue could be voted down.

※ ※ ※

Katie and Iris jingled the bell on the Mercantile's door, announcing their arrival.

"Good morning, ladies!" Liz called to them cheerfully.

"Hi, Liz! Can you have this small list ready for Jeremiah when he comes across from Samuel's in a bit? I don't think he will be long. He just wanted to see if Samuel had gotten a letter."

"Sure, I can." Liz took the list and briefly went over it to see if she had any questions. "Looks easy enough," Liz smiled at her friend and her sweet little girl. "You know, Mattie can't wait for Iris to come over and play today. Yesterday, all day long she planned what the girls were to play today." Liz giggled, thinking back on her little girl. "I hope she isn't too bossy with Iris, Sofie and Hope Rose today. She has it all in her head just as she thinks it should be."

Katie laughed, knowing the personalities of all the little girls. "Iris just thinks she should be one of the sisters—can't understand why she has to be home with the others in town."

"Well, I finally took down the old lace curtains we brought with us from Louisiana and put up some new cotton curtains I made. Since Abby's wedding, those lace curtains have turned into wedding play clothes. I don't know how many times we can play wedding, but those curtains have been the favorite for many days!"

Katie listened, imagining the fun of the day for the little girls. "I'm going to pick up a spool of quilting thread and take it with me. Please add it to the list."

"Oh, it can be my donation to the quilting since I will miss most of the day."

"Thanks, Liz. I wish you and Abby could come this morning. We will miss you, but we'll save some quilting for you this afternoon. I already told Abby so."

"Katie, you and Iris can go out the back door to the house. No reason to walk all the way around."

Katie picked up her basket, placed the spool of thread in it and led Iris out the back door.

"Good morning," Emma was cheery as she came out the back door of her restaurant.

"And to you," Katie called as she helped Iris down the step. They both watched Iris run to the porch of the Mailly home.

"I don't know who is more excited for the quilting—the little girls or the ladies," Emma said as she got in step with her friend Katie and walked the short way to the house.

"I guess regardless of our age, we enjoy the company of our friends and the adventure. My Iris has talked for days about when we come to Mattie and Sofie's house in town," Katie exclaimed. "Are you sure Hope Rose will stay all day too?" The questions between the two were endless.

"I suppose it has been a long spell for the four of them too," Emma replied, as she listened to her friend.

Megan had the house ready with the quilt frame set up. The backing for the quilt was sewn together, so it appeared as one large piece of cloth. The backing would be laid first on the frame with a large sheet of cotton batting placed on top of the backing. Anna Parker was first to arrive at the quilting since she had the quilt to be put in the frame. Anna unfolded the scrap Turkey-Tracks pieced top and stretched it out over the layer of cotton batting.

Megan put Lydia in her cradle and spread a light blanket over the sleeping baby. "Oh, Anna," she exclaimed, "the green border and sashing are just perfect for your scrap blocks." The two women worked, smoothing the three layers and pinning each section as they went.

"You surely love those long thin triangles and diamonds. I think they are in every quilt you make," Megan complimented her friend.

Anna had learned from her mother how to make a diamond shape then cut it up or use it whole to make beautiful blocks. The pattern appeared in every quilt her mother had made and somewhere in most of Anna's quilts also.

"Where did the green fabric come from?" Megan asked as she stretched the outside edges and pinned it to the fabric on the edge of the wooden quilt frame. She didn't recall it coming from the general store.

Anna stood and rubbed her lower back. "Tex brought a good length to me the last time he went to Austin."

Megan nodded, wondering if her friend was feeling well. "That was nice of him. Do we know where he is or what he is up to?"

"No, I haven't heard for sure, but I would guess he is with the political group, discussing the nominations and guessing what the Southern states will decide. This talk of secession is strong." Anna sat in a chair. As the women looked at each other silently, Anna said, "Are we ready to roll the quilt now?"

Rolling her side of the quilt to almost the middle, Megan said, "I'm sure it's important, and he is fine." She paused. "Let's try to keep the talk away from political news. We want to get away from our worries today."

Anna nodded her head in agreement as she rolled her side of the quilt.

Anna's little girl, Hope Rose, bounded through the doorway. She had insisted upon waiting on the porch for her friends to arrive. Mattie and Sofie were right behind her. Mattie stated, matter-of-factly, "Iris is here now. We will be playing on the porch." The three turned with the announcement and went back out the door, bounding down the steps all in chatter.

Katie released the hand of her youngest as Iris twisted to run ahead and meet the other little girls. The sounds of jumping and squealing filled the air. They were so excited for a day of play. Mattie gathered Iris, Hope Rose, and Sofie around a pint-sized table for tea and muffins.

Mattie glanced up as Emma and Katie came up the steps, laughing at the commotion the little ones were making. "We will be on the porch if you need us," she informed them.

"Well, thank you, Mattie, "Katie replied with her best tea-party manners. "Who has a new little wagon?" Katie remarked as she passed it at the bottom of the steps.

Emma looked back as she held the door open for Katie. "I'm not certain, but it sure is cute. They already have a couple of dolls loaded up in it."

"Why did we wait so long to get a quilting together?" Megan asked as she hugged and welcomed her two friends.

"I think it was wintertime and then you had a baby early and scared us all half to death!" Katie hugged Megan. "Then this thing called a prairie fire came along. We buried a good lady, had a wedding, sent Luke off to somewhere, and we haven't counted cougars or coyotes." Katie pulled a chair out at the frame, "I think that's a pretty full past several months."

"Speaking of coyotes," Anna asked, "Any news on Callie the cat? I hate to ask with the girls so close by," she looked to the open doorway and lowered her voice.

"Yes," Megan replied. "It hasn't been long enough to tell, but Lulu stitched up Callie and is keeping her at the cabin. The cat should have been dead from the encounter, but somehow, she is still with us."

Emma chuckled, "Well, if Mattie's prayers are as persistent with God as she is with us…"

The group started laughing, all knowing and loving Liz's girl Mattie.

Katie had about eight needles already threaded on the spool of thread. She took the spool in her left hand and loosely kept back seven needles as she pulled one needle and length of thread out and away from the spool. She nipped the thread with scissors and passed the threaded needle to Megan. Katie repeated the process for Anna, then Emma, and lastly, for herself. Then she put the spool with four threaded needles remaining threaded on the spool in the middle of the quilt top. Each woman knotted the end of her thread and slid the needle into the top layer of fabric, hiding the knot in the middle cotton layer.

Emma placed her left hand under the quilt top and leaned slightly over the frame. Taking the needle in her right hand, she slid one stitch under the top layer of fabric and pulled the thread gently to pop the knot at the end of the thread under the top layer. She checked to make sure it was smooth and nestled in the cotton fiber. Then she pushed the needle down into the quilt, slightly next to the first stitch. When she felt it with her finger under the quilt, her top hand gently pushed the needle to the left and up to the top of the fabric, then back down again, doing a rock and roll, back and forth with the needle. When the needle was full of stitches, it was pushed all the way through, and the needle and thread came through the layers of the quilt, making several tiny stitches that held the three layers together.

The women worked quietly at first, loading stitches on the needle then pulling the remaining thread through the pattern.

After a length of time Megan asked, "Emma, have you seen Chet lately? I don't recall seeing him in town."

"No, he hasn't been in town. I haven't seen him in several weeks. With everyone so busy, he's stayed at the ranch. They're down one cowboy now with Luke gone," she answered without really looking up.

"Last time he was in town, it was just a short visit at Abby's wedding. He seemed distant or upset; I wasn't sure which. You would have thought I couldn't boil water. He usually loves my food."

"Emma, you can make a sack taste good, and everyone knows that!" Katie remarked with a shake of her head. "I'd stop cooking for a man who didn't compliment me every now and then."

"Men aren't complicated, "Anna interjected, matter-of-factly. "We just make them out to be. Now, Emma, do you know any reason for Chet to be out of sorts with you?"

Emma stopped sewing and looked up with surprise. "No, we usually are—well, just friendly." She stumbled over her words.

Megan stopped her work and joined in. "Emma, have you or Chet ever talked about the future? Are you just friends? Maybe Chet wants more in a relationship?" Katie stopped sewing as well. Emma felt all eyes focused on her.

"I don't know what he wants. I'm happy being the only one not married. If he wants more, then I may have to find a new friend when I need a male chaperone."

"Just be careful, Emma," Katie warned. "You may be saying 'Shoo, cat, shoo' when someone else is saying, 'Here, kitty, kitty.'"

Emma sat up straighter and blinked a couple of times at her friends.

At that moment, Little Dove opened the front door of the Mailly home, and the voices of the little girls, who were giggling on the porch floated in with her. Little Dove had grown into a beautiful young woman with her dark, expressive eyes and long, dark hair, which today was braided and coiled slightly to one side on the back of her head.

Emma was happy to see her, abruptly ending the conversation. Truth be told, she was tired of trying to figure out Chet.

"Hi, everyone, "Little Dove greeted them. "Liz wanted me to tell Katie that Jeremiah took all the items on the list."

Katie nodded in approval at Little Dove. "Thank you."

"Emma, the ones you thought would come for breakfast did. They enjoyed your biscuits and took some cinnamon rolls with them for later. Luther Wheeler, the new smithy, said to tell you 'Hello,' that breakfast was good as always and that a lunch in a sack was perfectly acceptable. He said you should have a day off for quiltin'."

Emma smiled and laughed. Mr. Wheeler was a nice man, chatty, but never talked about himself. "Thank you, Little Dove. Did you take the sack lunches to Liz at the store?"

"Yes," the young woman replied. "She thought it was smart for you to have prepared meals for the unexpected."

"Perfect. Do you want to stay and quilt?" asked Anna, her adopted mother.

"Yes, but I told the little girls I would come back and have tea on the porch with them. They are having so much fun with those silly curtains. Poor Sofie had to walk the aisle three times before she got it right."

They all chuckled at the "wedding" taking place on the porch.

"Oh, I also told Liz I would help her some today."

"You are a much-needed worker today and always. Thank you!" Anna looked at her daughter who had come to her four years ago in need of a family. Tex was exactly right to steer her their way. At fifteen years of age, she was fast becoming a grown woman.

Liz popped over briefly at lunchtime to see how the work on the quilt was progressing. "Mr. and Mrs. Wilton were in town earlier this week," Liz commented. "He said Saturdays were just getting too busy, and he would continue to come during the week instead."

"What is it, Liz?" Katie inquired, seeing Liz was still contemplating some matter.

"I just feel sorry for Fanny Wilton."

"Why?" Katie asked again.

"She is a woman who cares about herself and her home. I know she can cook well. And she got another baby boy after her first little boy died when we first came to town, but she always seems so meek around her husband. She seems to be so grateful for all he does for her—like she doesn't deserve it."

Quietly, more to herself, Emma said, "Hmmm, more man trouble."

"What did you say?" Megan asked Emma to repeat her thought.

"Oh, nothing, you would just think that all of that would keep a man around long enough to be loved. Does he even love his wife?"

"I would think a foolish man would bring out the bad behavior in a woman or vice versa." Katie added her thoughts to the conversation.

"Today," Liz continued, "Fanny said she was purchasing kerosene to rub on her bedposts to keep insects from crawling up on the bed. She was also putting jar lids of water under each of the four bedposts, but only after she had tightened the ropes on the bed. Did you know to do that? I mean—about the spring remedies? Of course, everybody knows about tightening the ropes on the bed," Liz added. Anna didn't say a word to the others about Fanny's being a mail-order bride. She remembered the day they came to Parker to get married. She had been extremely shy and quiet. Anna guessed that Fanny didn't think she deserved anything.

The ladies stopped quilting long enough to eat lunch together, continuing to enjoy each other's company. After the little girls playing on the porch had been fed, Liz and Little Dove went back to work at the Mercantile. Sofie, the youngest of the little girls, started to cry. "What is it, honey?" her Aunt Megan asked and picked up the little girl who was now leaning on her lap.

"I don't want today to be over," she sniffled.

"Honey, don't be sad that it will be over. Be happy that today happened," Megan encouraged her and stroked Sofie's silky hair. Soon her eyes were shut, and Megan laid her on the bed for a nap.

Chapter 19

The afternoon wore away. The ladies stitched and chatted and unrolled the quilt as more of each section was completed. Anna stopped and stood for a moment, arching and stretching her back. Megan couldn't help but notice the contours of the round tummy showing through the skirt of her friend. Her eyes went up and met Anna's with a big smile.

Anna chuckled, "Well, I guess Megan is going to let the cat out of the bag."

"What, Megan?" Katie asked, looking at Megan then to Anna as to what the news would be.

"Me?" Megan replied coyly. "I think it's Anna's news."

All eyes went to Anna. She smiled and placed her hands on the fullness of her tummy.

"Yes, I think it's been long enough. I'm not going to be able to keep it quiet much longer. I can't believe I could have another baby. I lost a little boy after Hope Rose, but it's been a long while, and now, this one should arrive in the fall. You know, I usually don't talk about it 'til I'm pretty sure I can keep the baby growing." Anna beamed as she spoke of her new baby.

Katie looked at Anna, "I so hope you continue to feel well, and the baby can grow and be born into your family. Hope Rose will be so excited. We will be in prayer for you."

"I'm sorry about your little boy," Emma said with sympathy. She didn't know about this baby Anna had lost. She knew her friend had lost more babies than Emma could keep count of. Once again, she thought of marriage and babies and death—especially the deaths of people you love and even those you didn't get to know. "And, sweet Anna, why her?" Emma's question was a whisper to God.

※ ※ ※

Abby dismissed her students just a bit early. She wanted to get to the quilting as soon as she could. *The day has warmed to be a beautiful, Texas spring day,* she thought as she hurried to Liz's Mercantile. When she entered the general store, she noticed Little Dove and Liz were busy in different areas of the store. Liz looked up, spotted Abby and glanced at the clock on the wall.

"Oh, my! This day has flown by, Little Dove. I'm going with Abby to the house for the rest of the afternoon. Just let me know if you need help."

Little Dove nodded. "Yes, Miss Liz. I will."

Abby walked to the back door of the store and waited a moment for her cousin. Down the steps they went, chatting about their day as they started toward the house.

Liz watched with amusement as the little girls continued to play on the front porch. Mattie stood on the steps with a pan in her hand. Iris had a doll and placed it in the new wagon with her. Hope Rose and Sofie sat with the lace curtains draped around their shoulders, sipping tea at the tiny table on the porch.

When Mattie saw her mother and Aunt Abby, she started to run down the steps. Halfway down, she skidded to a stop and suddenly let out a blood-curdling scream. The ladies inside ran to the door, nearly upsetting the quilt frame. They stood on the porch, looking for Mattie and trying to figure out why she was continuing to scream. Liz and Abby started to run. As Liz came closer, she spotted the reason for her eldest's screams of terror. A large timber rattler had curled up underneath the little play wagon where Iris and her baby doll were sitting, completely unaware of the danger lurking below.

Liz knew immediately that the afternoon sun's rays of warmth directly below the porch and across the wagon had sent the rattler seeking shade. Iris noticed everyone looking at her and started to wiggle in the wagon, disturbing the coiled rattler. The snake raised its head and hissed.

The wagon's shaking *above* the snake, Mattie's screaming in *front* of the snake and the group of frightened women's *surrounding* the snake effectively prevented the predator from retreating. The alarmed snake began to posture and prepare to strike! If Iris stepped out of the wagon, the snake might strike her. Even worse, seeking a way of escape, the snake could even crawl up into the low wagon.

What to do? Liz thought. Taking control of the situation, Liz began issues orders. "Mattie, stand still!" Liz commanded her daughter. "Iris," she firmly called, "Be very still, honey. Don't move. We are going to get you."

"Ladies," Liz called out, "Anyone have a gun?"

"We do in the house, but it's not a pistol. Iris will be injured." Megan sighed.

"Okay, think quickly, ladies." Liz didn't take her eyes off the snake. "I'll keep the snake's attention. Emma, can you go behind the post, hang on the porch rail, grab Iris and swing her up and away from the wagon?"

"Yes," Emma answered as she scurried over to the side out of the harried snake's view. "Anna, hang on to me!"

"Mattie, you're doing good. Be really still, honey. In a minute, I'm going to tell you to hurry back to the porch."

Big tears rolled down Mattie's cute, chubby cheeks. As she looked at her mother, she scarcely nodded, letting her know she understood.

Jodi Barrows

"Iris, you are doing good, honey. Emma's going to help you!" Liz knew she still had the snake's attention as it coiled into a defensive stance and continued to vigorously shake its rattle. She maintained a constant distance of the length of the rattler, staying out of reach should it launch itself in an instantaneous thrust at her, trying to strike her. "Abby, go back to the mercantile and get my Colt at the register."

Abby obeyed immediately, turning without a word and running toward the store.

"Emma, I'm going to get the snake to strike at me. You grab Iris when I do."

Liz pulled a length of fabric slowly from the basket, draping it across her arm. Keeping a tight hold on one end, she hurled the long piece of cloth at the snake. The angry rattler struck immediately, catching the fabric with its fangs.

As Emma reached for Iris, Katie quickly reached down and pulled the terror-stricken Mattie back onto the porch. Hope Rose hid behind her mother's skirt, waiting for Mattie.

Emma lunged out, pulling Iris from the wagon and dragging her across the porch railing.

The plan of action seemed to work quickly and seamlessly. Everyone had waited for the snake to lunge at Liz before taking action. But the unexpected happened… Liz stumbled as she pulled the fabric back toward her. Only then did she realize that the rattler's fangs had snagged the material, and even as she pulled the cloth toward her, she was also draggling the snake toward her! Liz screamed, taking a few running steps backward as she let go of the cloth. As she retreated, she bumped into Abby who had returned with her Colt.

Instead of handing Liz the Colt, Abby took a steady aim, pulled the trigger, and dirt shot up from the ground only inches from the snake. The aggravated rattler, which had now freed itself from the cloth, coiled to strike a second time at both Liz and Abby. The gun flashed again as Abby pulled the trigger, this time, hitting the snake. A third shot rang out, finishing the job.

Liz and Abby stumbled to each other, and Liz enveloped her shaking cousin in her arms. Abby's breath was uneven and hot against her shoulder. Only silence and the acrid smell of gunpowder lingered.

"Abby…Liz," Megan frantically shrieked as she took a few steps off the porch and ran toward them, passing the huge, dead snake, still writhing in its death dance.

Sofie, bread crumbs on her face, toddled to the middle of the porch, having missed all of the commotion. "Momma?" she asked and looked about. Emma put her hands around Sofie's waist and lifted her up.

"She's okay, honey. Everyone is fine."

No one felt like quilting any more. The day of fun had come to a bizarre ending. As the women gathered their little girls, they all retreated into the house. Emma slammed the front door hard and looked out the window on the door like she expected another vicious attack at any moment. Then she turned the lock, bolting the door as if to declare "No more trouble today!"

Chapter 20

June 1860

Luke had now been gone for months, and Chet sorely missed him. He always had a way of perking things up. *Why did he have to go and leave?* Chet wondered. His dry sense of humor, matter-of-fact ways and good looks drew a crowd, and fun times were always to be had.

Sitting on the back of his horse, watching the herd of dirty livestock, Chet pondered what he wanted—really wanted. After his pa had died, he had drifted around. His mother had sold the land they had ranched and had taken his little sisters back east where they lived close to her side of the family. He had met the Mailly clan as he was drifting through Louisiana and worked at their timber mill. Then he had followed them with their dreams back to Texas. He didn't know how to dream big on his own like the Mailly clan did. His old boss Lucas had always said, "Love God, dream big, work hard and never, never give up." The words of this man were branded into his brains.

The low moan of the whipping wind caught his attention and ruffled his hair that topped his collar. Last time he saw Emma she had threatened to cut it. But he was liking it kinda long. After all, his friend Colt, the sheriff in Birdville, had really long hair. He took his hat off and wiped his face, streaking the dirt that had mixed with his sweat on the hot day.

"Is this what I want?" he asked himself. Chet had never asked these questions of himself before. He had always just drifted along, not really ever having a plan. He liked his horse and working for the

Rolling M ranch, and he liked running the freight for the Mercantile on occasion. Liz and Thomas paid him well. And, Emma? *Well, I like Emma too,* he thought, *even though she is a handful, but then, what girl worth having isn't?* He thought some more while watching the longhorns graze on the grass.

Chet liked breaking horses and was good at it. *I love a good horse,* he thought, as he patted the spare pony he rode today. Thomas had many fine horses, and Chet was able to choose any horse he pleased from the herd each day. That herd was a sight too pretty for a man to look upon. The wranglers knew exactly how to gentle the horses and ready them for breaking. Luke had broken the most difficult one, but he had the best of them in Thunder. "That Thunder shore was a beauty. I shore wish Luke was around. I wouldn't feel so low," Chet told his horse as he patted her soft neck.

Chet thought more about all that he had learned from Jackson since he had joined the cowboys at the ranch. That Ranger knew how to break a horse the Comanche way. He had passed on those skills to Thomas and a few others at the ranch. Because of Jackson, he had thought about signing up with those Rangers until the government had disbanded them. *Integrity, courage, and honor—that was to be admired.* He would have liked to own one of those Sam Walker Colts—*Now, that's a gun!*

His thoughts carried him to Luke again and how Luke was carrying America's information across half the continent, binding a nation together with his Pony Express work. That job sure had its allure—a proud partnership between horse and rider. The stories fascinated the population, and the newspapers were full of stories. Luke hadn't been afraid to act on his dreams.

Chet, deep in his thoughts, continued to weave his way through the dancing heat waves. He needed to make up his mind about

Emma. He was sure that filly could be broken, but he wasn't sure that was what he wanted to do.

The moan he heard this time wasn't the wind, but a spring calf caught in the thicket. He climbed down from his horse to help free the little creature. After the calf was out and went bawling to his momma, Chet stopped to dust himself off and took a good look at himself. He was a good cowboy; in fact, he was great at it. He pulled the loose, dusty hair from across his face and looked down. Worn clothing, scuffed boots and all his money locked away in his room at the bunkhouse. *What am I saving my money for anyway?*

He mounted the unnamed horse and remembered what Tex had said to him. "Your kindness or cruelty can be made known by the way you leave a trail."

"Just what kind of trail am I leaving?" he asked out loud. "Just dirt and sweat, I guess. My life's blowing here and there like the wind."

Chet pushed his hat down firmly and took a swallow of water from his canteen. Yep, I need to talk to Emma and get some things settled with that girl. *That's why I'm feeling out of sorts. If I can get that settled, my life will be better.* With more confidence, he mounted his horse and nudged her sides as they trotted to the other side of the herd.

Chapter 21

"I miss Luke," Mattie suddenly stated as she sat with a pencil in her hand. The page below her hand had numbers all written in rows exactly like her mother's ledger book. "We get letters on the stagecoach for people here. Why can't the letters that Luke has just go on a stagecoach?"

Liz stopped writing in her own ledger book. The sales at her Mercantile continued to grow daily. Wagon train loads of people pushing west and the trail drivers of dusty cattle heading north were now a weekly occurrence. Fort Worth and all it had to offer, good or bad, was a draw for the weary traveler. Fort Worth was gaining popularity as being the place where the West began.

She missed her only son and sighed, "I know, sweetheart. Me, too. I wish we had a way to hear from him and know that he has made it safely to the Horseshoe Creek Station."

"Where is that?" Mattie asked. "Is it on that big map you have?" Mattie stood and went to her mother's side.

They both looked at the large map of the United States that Liz had nailed to the wall. Mostly her freight wagon roads and depo stops were marked though she had added the stage line trails and, lastly, her post-office stations.

"I have been waiting for a government letter to tell me where and when to add the Pony Express mail stations, but I haven't received one. Congress can't seem to agree on adding them as a government contact."

Mattie looked at her mother, trying to understand her words. Liz realized Mattie didn't understand, so she made another attempt to explain. "The men who make our laws and rules and bills at our Capitol have to do some more work."

"Okay," Mattie replied quickly, "if they are behind, they have to work faster then."

"Yes." Liz sighed again and slowly nodded her head. "From what I can tell, Horseshoe Creek is almost straight north from us." She picked up Mattie and stood her on a bench so she could see the map better. Liz placed her finger on the map where they were and ran her finger up and over to where she thought Luke was.

"It's…a…long…ways." Mattie dragged the words out as she looked at the location where her brother was hoped to be. "Has he made it?"

"He should have made it just in time." Liz helped Mattie back down to the floor. "In fact, I'm hoping," she paused, "that every time the stage comes in that we have a newspaper with a report on the Pony Express's work."

"Do you think he has any stories of his own about snakes or coyotes?" Mattie's eyes grew wide as she leaned forward with her arms outstretched. She was thinking about her own stories and sharing them with her brother.

"Oh, I'm sure he does—maybe even an outlaw or an Indian one too!" Liz teased Mattie, but hoped in the back of her mind that his trip was boring with no stories of his own to tell! But she knew better in her heart. She prayed every day for the safety and return of her oldest child. "I hope you remember to pray for Luke. I'm positive that he appreciates your thinking of him."

"Do you think he has some new friends at the station?" Mattie looked quizzical at her mother who was still standing close by.

Threads of Courage

"Yes, why do you ask?" Liz wrinkled her brow, tilting her head, amazed at how her little girl thought about matters in such detail.

"I think Chet is real sad and doesn't have any new friends since Luke left. I don't want Luke to be sad like Chet." Mattie's lip puckered out a little.

"Sweetheart, why do you think Chet is sad?" Liz's mind was now a million miles from her work in her ledger book. She had been figuring how much extra to buy of various supplies. Some of her inventory had been hard, if not nearly impossible, to get with the rumblings of war. Trying to get equivalents to stock was time-consuming and costly. She also wanted a good back stock if her supply chain shut down completely. At least, the daily goods were stocked on her shelves and in her storage areas.

"I heard him in the barn with his horse. I was in the loft with the new kittens." Mattie had Liz's full attention. She silently nodded to encourage her to continue with her story.

"I thought he was crying. I never saw Luke or any of the ranch hands cry, so I peeked through a crack and moved some hay to see better. He was brushing his horse down and said he sure did miss Luke and Emma, and he was lonely as a polecat. Momma?" she asked and stopped with a puzzled look, "where did Emma go that he missed her? I see her every day."

She looked at the door that pointed toward "Emma's Table" next door. About that same time, Emma came through, drying her hands on a towel then tucking it into her apron.

"Hi, ladies!" Emma greeted them. The wood floor squeaked as she walked closer to the two. Reaching into her apron pocket, she pulled out a few oatmeal cookies, still warm from the oven.

"Emma, have you been somewhere, and we didn't miss you?" Mattie quizzed her as she reached up for the cookies.

Emma chuckled and looked from Mattie to Liz, handing her a cookie too. "No, not that I know of, just back and forth on that worn path from the front door of the house to the back door of the work kitchen. I don't think I've even visited dreamland often enough."

Mattie listened carefully while munching on her snack. She seemed satisfied for the present and turned back to her practice of numbers.

Emma stepped closer to Liz. "What's up with Mattie? Seems like a serious conversation you two were involved in." She leaned on Liz's desk and looked down at Liz's book of numbers.

"Emma…" Liz thought that now was a good time to ask about Chet, "Are you having any problems with Chet? Mattie seemed to think Chet is sad about you and Luke being away. He misses you both."

Emma arched her eyebrow, tilted her head, and did the Mailly "bite-the-edge-of-your-lip" thing that most of the women did when confused or worried. "Well, yes, we had a conversation a few days ago. He had ridden into town at an odd time and found me cooking alone at the restaurant. I didn't know what to think about his visit and thought it best to rest on it a while. I hoped or thought it would ease out. I had no idea he was distraught over it or even dragged it to the next day. I could tell he was all in a frizz about something, but I'm still confused about the whole encounter myself."

"I remember some talk at the quilting."

Emma continued, "I don't know what got him thinking about us a couple, you know—more than just good friends and kinda, well, family." The woman with curly hair and emerald eyes paused and looked at Liz. "Do you or did you think we were a couple? 'Cause he seemed to think everyone did, and he felt pressured to 'stake his claim on me before someone else did.'

"I told him there was no need as we were just fine. Chet asked if I had a sweetheart at some other ranch or here in town," Emma continued. "I replied with a strong and flat 'no'! He then asked, 'Well, do you want to get married?' I turned to look at him, and he was now standing in front of me. I said, 'Why would we want to do that? We haven't even kissed!' He grabbed me by my shoulders and kissed me—not much of a kiss as you would expect at a proposal, I might add. I must admit that I was slightly bewildered at his actions. I replied, 'Do you want married life with me right now, Chet?' He paused and stepped back from me, almost worried of what I would say. 'Well, no, I don't know. Do we?' he said back to me, and he sounded so confused. I've never seen him without confidence. It's like he was a scolded little boy."

Liz covered her mouth, afraid that a giggle might creep out.

"Don't laugh. He was so serious," Emma added with concern for her friend.

"I'm sorry," Liz straightened her face. "Then what happened?"

"I said, 'No, I don't want or need to get married. Do you?' He blinked and looked at me, and I couldn't tell what he was thinking. I don't think he really wanted to get married, do you?" She didn't wait for Liz's answer before continuing with her story. "'Chet, you work at the ranch, and I work in town. We are both happy doing that, aren't we?' He mumbled something and walked out the door—just rode away. I think he came into town just to talk with me about this, but our talk only left me more confused."

Liz paused for a moment, thinking. "Thomas said back months ago, well, when they were hunting the mountain lion and Lydia was born, that Chet was in a state of confusion with you."

"Why? Nothing changed that I know about. We are good friends who enjoy each other's company with friends and family. We eat, laugh, and talk over life in our town. We are there for each other when we need it. That's not married life." Just as Emma finished the words, she looked at Liz. "Oh, Liz, what am I gonna do? He does want to get married. I didn't think he was serious when I said 'No.' No wonder he is sad. What pushed him to ask me, and at that point, like that?" She sank into Liz's desk chair.

"Thomas said that Chet saw you with someone else on the boardwalk and that you seemed to be really happy to see that other cowboy."

"Who?" Emma asked, "Which one? If he only knew how many cowboys or single men, in general, I talk to each week. If I wanted or needed to get married, I could have a thousand times or more. Poor Chet! What am I to do?"

Liz felt sorry for them both. Not that long ago she had felt pushed into marriage. It certainly hadn't been without issue either. Being in town at work and on the ranch both in a week's time was not easy to manage. Finally, she and Thomas had found a way to make their working relationship function. But now with Megan's not working and being a full-time mom, the situation had become more difficult again. *There just isn't enough of me in a day to make everyone happy.* Liz sighed over the conundrum she faced in life.

Chapter 22

AUGUST 1860

Tex was finally back in Fort Worth with news from the Capitol, and he requested Samuel to call a town meeting of the men on the following Saturday afternoon. As word spread over the following week, the anxiety levels grew among the men and women of the county.

"This political tension is about to get the best of me," Abby stated. "Samuel has been wound tight as a new pocket watch all summer."

With that day now upon them, the women had gathered in the Mercantile where they could see Samuel's office. With the heat of the day, the doors were open and, hopefully, some of the voices and statements could be heard clearly as they floated in.

The women knew as well as the men what was at stake with this election. It would be the pivotal point on Southern states seceding from the Union. They were proud and determined to be able to keep the right of the state to choose and make decisions for their state's good. No president, Congress or "for the good of the Union" would be the final word.

"Can you tell us anything about what Samuel or Tex knows?" Katie Longmont asked. Because of being on the ranch for most of the summer, she had heard very little on the political unrest. Jeremiah had only been making sporadic and hasty trips to town, as needed.

Most of the ranching or farming families were too busy in the warm months; crops and animals needed too much tending. But everyone in the nation knew the heat from the Capitol wasn't all about the weather. Most of the women stood silent or shook their heads "No."

One hundred or more men had arrived in town to hear the news. Some paced or visited on the boardwalk of Samuel's office. They were waiting in the street, leaning on or sitting in wagons, and in general, all over the area. Word had spread almost as quickly as a prairie fire that the conventions were over; candidates had been chosen and, now the battle for votes was beginning. No doubt, this political season had been the most heated that any could remember. But much was at stake, and much was riding on every word that was spoken.

Samuel and Tex along with Jackson, Thomas and Jeremiah all came out of Samuel's law office and stepped onto the wood porch in front of the office. The crowd hushed to a silence where a pin could be heard if it were dropped.

The women hushed each other, straining to hear also. Abby, Liz and Katie went to stand at the open door of the Mercantile just outside on the porch. Men were also standing up and down the board sidewalk on the Mercantile side of the street.

Katie nodded at Liz and motioned for her to look up the street to the other end of town where the saloons and gambling dens had started to pop up. Cowboys and drifters were hurriedly coming their way. Liz saw Mr. Barton coming too. For a moment, she wondered how he was getting his whiskey. With so much on her mind, Liz had forgotten about him. He locked eyes with her but neither smiled in greeting. Right then, Samuel started to speak, and they both looked his way.

"As we all know, this is an election year, and much is weighing in the balance for our country. Tex has spent most of this year in Austin with Governor Sam Houston."

Tex stepped forward as his named was mentioned. First, he smiled and looked toward the Mercantile where the female population was gathered. "The good news is that the first child has been born in the Governor's mansion a few days ago. The new baby boy, Temple Houston, and his parents are all doing well!"

Cheers were heard from the crowd. The women clapped and whispered to each other.

"Now to the critical news at hand," Tex started again. "Governor Houston strongly implores us to keep a cool head, make sound decisions as we roll into this election period and not to let our pride run away with us. Texans are fighting men—not afraid to go into the gates of hell. With that said, we are to go about our work and grow our crops and animals and families.

"Governor Houston does not want Texas to secede if political tensions rise. He does not want the State to feel pressured to leave the Union. He will not vote for the State to secede. Now Mr. Smith will fill us in on the political news."

The time they all feared had now arrived, and the tension in the crowd was felt by everyone. The reality and seriousness of what Tex had said rolled over in their thoughts. Trying to sort it out, they waited for more news.

"Let me update you all with the political news and where our nation now sits. In April, the Democrats held a convention in Charleston; the first platform, which was pro-slavery, was rejected in a vote. Eight states walked out, forcing the convention to adjourn. They could not agree on a candidate for the presidential election."

The crowd remained silent, allowing Samuel to finish telling all that he knew.

"The Republicans held their convention in Chicago in May. Lincoln was nominated on the third ballot, defeating William Seward.

At that time, he stood as a moderate on the issue of slavery. The Republican Party insisted on leaving slavery alone in the states where it already existed, but stood against the spread of it to the new territories and states. We all know the push of territories west will shift the playing field on votes in Congress."

The citizens of Fort Worth looked at each other and nodded in agreement.

Katie leaned over to Abby. "Maybe this isn't as bad as we thought."

"I hope you're right. "Abby sighed but thought it was wishful thinking on her part.

"The Democrats reconvened in June in Baltimore and chose Stephen Douglas as the nominee, but the Southern Democrats walked out again, unhappy with the new choice for nominee."

"Well, they should have," one man in the crowd called out. "We all know Lincoln ate Douglas up in those debates in '58. Douglas could not make a decision if his life depended on it."

The crowd agreed, unable to hold their silence in agreement any longer.

"Gentlemen, gentlemen," Samuel raised his hands to calm and quiet the crowd. "We now have a Southern Democratic Party, and their nominee is John C. Breckinridge." A murmur of approval rippled through the crowd as most liked the man.

"And not let us forget the Whigs, the 'Old Gentlemen's Party.' The Constitutional Unionists have nominated John Bell."

"That's no problem," an unnamed man in the crowd yelled out. "They are the Know-Nothing Party anyway!"

"Four parties are what we have with the Democrats splitting," Tex added, stepping up next to Samuel again. He started talking with a loud voice over the noise of the crowd. "Lincoln is campaigning in the Southern states on a moderate position. He is a respected state politician. Let's give him a chance and see what he says. When he said, 'A house divided against itself cannot stand,' he was right."

"What do we do now?" another man from the crowd asked loudly.

"We will wait to see what unfolds and do as Governor Houston said. We are to go about our work, grow our crops and take care of our families and animals. Remember Sam Houston wants to stay with the Union."

"We are Texans first!" the same man yelled out.

"And we are Americans foremost," Samuel firmly said. "We Texans are fiercely independent and proud people, and we have poured out our blood creating this state—fighting outlaws, Indians, criminals and governments. Look across our landscape, and you will see the log cabins of Kentucky, Mexican mud or German rock and wood homes, small Southern plantations, or homes from New York and the East. We are pieced together like the quilts our womenfolk make—each piece intricately placed in solid unity with each other. We must not let the political uncertainty unravel our seams or tear us apart. Together we will stand as Texans and as Americans."

The men nodded their heads again and began to talk among themselves.

Samuel stepped back, signaling he was done reporting. He turned to Thomas. "I guess that went well enough."

"It was only information—nothing to be decided upon yet." Thomas patted Samuel on the back, reassuring him of a job well done. "We have done all we can do for the time at hand."

Liz watched the crowd disperse to their wagons and start down the road. The heaviness in her soul couldn't be shaken. *In only a matter of time, a decision will have to be made, and the outcome will divide friends, families and, finally, a nation. Grandfather was right.* The time was now upon them with the presidential election.

❀ ❀ ❀

The summer days passed, and fall was upon Ft. Worth. The community had their seasonal rituals as the crops that had been planted were now harvested. Women canned their gardens' produce for provisions during the winter and the early spring months. People came and went in the Mercantile and through town. A wagon train stopped for a few days as repairs were made. The men traded political news, and the women tried not to worry over what they were not supposed to hear or understand. But the dividing of the Union was on everyone's mind. Some joined the wagon train to travel farther west to get away while others simply hid their head in the sand as they had for years, ignoring what wasn't on their doorstep.

❀ ❀ ❀

Before long, Thomas walked into the Mercantile with Liz and Mattie. As soon as he sat down at the back of the store where she played and ran her part of the general store, Mattie jumped on his lap.

"Daddy, I missed you!" Mattie hugged his neck with both of her arms, squeezing him tight. Then she placed a kiss on his clean-shaven cheek.

When Liz finally had a moment when the store was free of customers, she stood leaning against the counter, watching father and daughter interact. Thomas was so good with his little girls. She knew he missed them because he had been staying in town more since the birth of Lydia. Life was good when it revolved around the time Daddy would get home.

"I've missed you too, little one," Thomas hugged her tightly. "I have good news for you, Mattie."

Mattie leaned back on his lap and placed her hands on each side of his face, commanding his full attention. "What, Papa? What?" she squealed as she looked into his face. Thomas looked at Liz, drawing her into the conversation.

Liz was now inquisitive about what the good news could possibly be. She certainly needed some. She smiled, continuing to watch the two.

"Mattie, your prayers have been answered. Against all odds, your Callie cat is going to be just fine—without one of her ears. She healed up pretty quickly with Lulu's doctoring, and the really great news is that she is past her quarantine time of having rabies. We will let her loose on the ranch when I get home."

"Oh, Daddy!" she squealed again and jumped down to dance and hop in her excitement. "Can I see her when I get home?" She clapped in delight.

"Yes, Sweetheart, you can. You must have prayed real hard 'cause Callie should have died in the attack or contracted the disease."

Liz smiled. "She prayed every day and often. Mattie is a good little prayer warrior. Thank you, Thomas, for giving the cat a chance and not putting it down right away. I am sure Lulu did a wonderful job of nursing her back to health."

"She did," he chuckled. "I checked the cat twice a day. At any sign of rabies, I was going to put her down. Probably really shouldn't have taken such a chance…" he paused, "if the girls had been around the ranch, I wouldn't have." Thomas said seriously and then chuckled once again. "I think nursing the cat gave Lulu something to dote on with you and the girls gone."

Liz moved closer as Thomas stood and reached out to draw her into his embrace. "Sure has been quiet with all my girls gone. I've missed you!"

"Me too. I've missed you so much!" Liz kissed him. "We will try to get a schedule and some more help now that Megan and Lydia are out of the woods and completely healthy again. Just a weekend or an overnight is not enough for me, Thomas," Liz sighed, looking at her handsome, understanding husband.

"I agree." He kissed her again and held her close. "Mattie and I are going over to the house to see Sofie and the others. You about to close up?"

"Yes," Liz answered as she considered her work. "I won't be but a few minutes. Tell Megan we can start supper."

Mattie waited patiently at the back door of the mercantile for her papa to take her hand. "Okay," Thomas said as he took Mattie's little hand. "Abby and Samuel are coming over too. Jeremiah and his family are eating at the Parkers tonight."

As father and daughter headed down the steps, Mattie said, "You love Momma; I'm glad you love her." They paused a moment as he bent down to acknowledge her words at her eye level.

"Yes, I do," Thomas said, wondering where her thoughts were going. "You girls and your mother are my family. I miss you."

"Chet misses Emma too!" Mattie stated firmly. "But Emma doesn't love Chet, and he's sad. I'm glad you aren't sad, Papa."

Thomas listened to his little girl's grownup thoughts. She heard and listened to everything around her. "I'm sorry Chet and Miss Emma are having problems of some kind. Now that Callie is well, let's pray for Chet and Miss Emma."

"But Papa," she replied seriously, "God has time for all of our prayers." She emphasized all with her face and hands.

Thomas smiled at the wisdom of his little daughter. "Yes, He does, Mattie. You are so smart to know that." He stood as Mattie pulled his hand, skipping to the steps of the porch.

※ ※ ※

Daily life continued as the November voting date drew closer.

Threads of Courage

Every newspaper that came into the Mercantile was read from cover to cover by every man and woman, gleaning every bit of information they could and hanging on to every word.

Liz and her family were happy as their life settled down after their excitement of new babies, animal attacks and the community prairie fires. Life was returning to their normal days of enjoying family and working together.

With the help of a few others, Samuel and Tex built a sheriff's office and jail located on the same side of the street as the law office but away from the Mercantile, the church and the school. Jackson had finally accepted the job of town sheriff. He spent most of his time over the rise where the gambling hall had been built and where the cattle-drive cowboys taking the Chisholm Trail stopped to rest their cattle and wet their whistle.

Some of the cowboys would mosey down the street to the Mercantile for a bar of Mailly soap or for a good meal at Emma's Table. Some of the drunken, unruly cowboys would spend the night in the jail with Emma delivering breakfast to the now-sober and passive occupants. Emma pretty much knew everything that was happening in town from the law office, the jail occupants, the patrons of the gambling halls, the cowboys and the general store customers. She wasn't a gossip though, refusing to share all she knew with any who would listen.

Town was full again on Election Day in November. The news of Lincoln's victory wasn't long in coming.

※ ※ ※

The winded pony stopped abruptly in front of the Pony Express stationhouse. Luke waited for the rider to jump off so he could grab the mochila with the letters and newspapers, which announced Abraham Lincoln as the new President of the Union.

"Did you hear?" the rider called out as he approached Luke and jumped from the tired horse.

"No," Luke quickly replied. He tossed the mochila into place over the fresh horse. Luke vaulted onto the back of the black horse as the rider exclaimed, "Pass the word: Lincoln's our new President. The letters and articles are in your mochila."

Luke snapped the reins over the horse and was off at full speed in less than two minutes from the other rider's arrival. Suddenly, he was struck with the realization of exactly what he was carrying across country to the West. He carried not just any newspaper or letter from home but the official news of the United States government and the announcement of the victor of the presidential race. Luke's heart beat faster, and the pounding hooves stirred up the trail dust as he pushed his pony harder.

Each rider did his best over the two-thousand-mile trail to announce the election results in the fastest time. A new record was set—only six days to tell the West who their new leader would be!

Chapter 23

December 1860

"Any news?" Thomas asked as the men assembled after church. Being at the ranch most of the time and with Jackson in town all of the time, Thomas felt out of the loop on the most current news. Liz filled him in on what the newspapers reported, and then he read them from cover to cover. Still, he knew Samuel was a wealth of up-to-date Texas news, which greatly concerned him.

Samuel added another log to the fire as the day was cold and dreary. His friends—usually Jackson, Jeremiah, and Pastor Parker—liked to sit around to talk in his living area above his office. Today though, Parker was home with his wife and new baby. The community considered this group of five to possess wisdom, cool tempers, and good decision-making skills to lead the community. Any time Tex was in town, he joined the group as well as he usually had the most current news coming from the Capitol.

Samuel sat back down and picked up his coffee cup. "I just learned from Tex earlier this week that Indian raids are on the rise, and trying to move them to the designated Indian Territory north of us has presented problems. Some resent the western progression of the settlers, ranchers and wagon trains."

"Well, if we don't worry over our own government unrest, we can worry about the Indian raids on our ranchers. I almost forgot about them with the South in its own upheaval." Jeremiah leaned forward and rubbed his hands together in front of the fire, which had started to come to life from the addition of the logs.

Thomas chuckled at Jeremiah's sentiment, but he only said what everyone else was thinking. "What else, Samuel?"

"Lt. Colonel Robert E. Lee and four companies of the 2nd Cavalry have been deployed way south at Brownville to end the cross-border raids by Texans and Mexicans."

"It never ends does it?" Thomas sighed.

"No," Jackson agreed. "But it has given me my life's work. I rode with Lee for a while 'til I was assigned to meet a group of wagons on the East Texas border. That's where we met the Mailly women and brought them on to Fort Worth. My work is to no liking of Megan, I might say."

Jackson noted, "A few Texas Rangers have gone with Sully Ross and a detachment of the 2nd Cavalry to the Peace River not too far from here."

"Ya, they were asking for volunteers to go with them," Thomas said. "They came by the ranch, but we had no warm bodies to give as we are down to the bone; I can't get a full day's work out of Chet." Thomas joked at the last statement as everyone knew that Chet and Emma were on the outs, but no one understood why. Chet didn't go into town much and seemed quite content to take any extra shifts.

The door burst open downstairs, and Tex and Pastor Parker took the staircase two steps at a time. They burst into the room with a barrage of energy and out of breath.

"I rode ahead to tell Parker," the old Ranger was out of breath and took a moment to recover. He looked over the men, mentally taking note of who was gathered in the room.

Parker stepped closer to the fire and brushed a few raindrops from his hat. "Tell 'em, Tex."

"I was riding with the group that went out to the Peace River to look for the Comanche. We had a fairly peaceful raid as raids go, and we found a blue-eyed squaw. We thought something was amiss and tried to figure out what it was. We tried to get her to speak English, but she acted like she didn't know any—speaking only Comanche and looking like an Indian. Anyway, we brought them in—her and her baby girl named Prairie Flower. She also has an older son named Quanah. They are holding her at Birdville. Colt is handling some of the things, trying to notify as many families as possible. I came here to tell Parker that Cynthia Ann has been found well, alive, and married to the chief's son Nocona. She has several children. Twenty-six years have passed since that little girl was captured at the Parker Fort on the Navasota River.

The men stood silent, all astounded by the news.

"Just wait 'til the women hear about this!" Jackson exclaimed.

※　※　※

"Lincoln is a known opponent to slavery, and neither does he want war," Liz said to the gathering of ladies at the quilt frame. She pulled her needle and thread through the patch to quilt it and stopped. "The South Carolina legislature perceives Lincoln and his conviction on slavery as a threat. They are calling a state meeting to vote to secede from the Union."

"The ink wasn't even dry on the ballots when they started making plans," Katie said with disapproval. "Even their Governor Pickens said they would go before the election. As the third richest in the Union, the state representatives felt they had a lot of political power. Jeremiah was quite upset, knowing a domino fall would come next." "Only more will follow, putting more pressure on Texas to secede also. The hill country group is the only area that wants to stay with the Union. In that case, the Texas vote will go for seceding and joining the Confederacy of Southern States," Liz voiced her thoughts, still not stitching along the marked seam line.

The rain, tapping on the window, was the only noise in the room after Liz had spoken. It was a Sunday afternoon, and word had spread quickly at church that things were coming to a volatile point.

"What other states will follow South Carolina and join the Confederacy?" asked Little Dove as she wasn't as knowledgeable on the states' affiliations as were the other women.

Megan spoke first. "I feel relatively sure our Louisiana and Mississippi will secede as well, both being slave states. Alabama, Florida and Georgia will come along too. They all want the right as a state to make decisions for the State."

The room remained quiet for a few minutes as each quilter was lost in her own thoughts and concerns. Liz went back to her needle and loaded stitches on it with the up-and-down rocking of the needle. Each time she pushed the needle down, her fingers underneath the quilt felt it, and she tipped the needle back up through the layers of cotton. When the process was repeated several times with the rocking motion of the needle, more stitches were placed on the needle. Then she pulled all of the needle and thread taut in the fabric and started all over again. Twelve stitches per inch was excellent, and everyone present could do the expected twelve.

"I miss Anna; wish she and baby, Aubrey Faith, could come today," Katie said. "If the rain and cold weather wasn't here, I'm sure she would have felt up to it. Both of them are getting along quite well. I was hoping to hold and spoil that little bundle of joy."

"I just love the smell of a new baby," sighed Megan, "so pure and sweet, innocent and untouched."

"As far as I know," Emma added, "they had an easy time, and Anna did quite well. Little Aubrey came fast. Without saying a word, each female knew that a live, healthy baby was a gift for any of them, but especially for Anna."

"I'm so happy for her," Abby added to everyone's sentiments.

Little Dove was quilting away, simply listening and learning. She didn't have the maturity of the other quilters as of yet, but she was accepted among them as an adult woman. Her own experience had taught her well at her young age. "Yes, her water broke and her labor started, and within an hour, we had our baby. Hope Rose is just a sweet, good, big sister, and Parker won't leave her side. He insisted on staying with her today and pushed me with my cape and hood right out the door in the rain."

"Wasn't she born after midnight on Tuesday a week ago, barely making it into December?" Katie asked, not sure she knew all of the details of Anna's story.

"Yes," Little Dove replied in a pleased voice. Her Indian accent wasn't as apparent as it had been from years ago. "The baby came so fast we didn't have time to call anyone for help. For all of the hardship she has had, this birth was very simple and easy."

"Well, she deserved one and had put her time in, for sure," Katie replied to Little Dove.

All of the women had been over at some time during the week to see Anna and her baby and offer any help they could. But with Little Dove right there, there wasn't much need. The cold and wet weather had kept many away from town for the weekend, so not much news was circulating. Things were fairly quiet except for the lingering thoughts on the splitting of a nation and what could develop. The women had all steered clear of talking about it that day, but the apprehension weighed heavily upon each one.

Chapter 24

Christmas Eve 1860

Emma poured popcorn into a bowl. The little girls each took a piece and pushed it on the needle and then slid it down a string as the popcorn roping began to form.

"Careful, Sofie, don't poke your fingers," Liz warned her youngest daughter as she helped her guide the flake onto the needle. Mattie, you are doing very well."

"Can I put it on the Christmas tree when I'm done?" Mattie asked but never removed her concentration from threading the popcorn flakes.

"Yes, you may," Liz smiled. Her little girl was growing up and so excited for the Christmas season.

Emma sat down, picked up another needle and started pushing cranberries on it. The red juice ran down her fingers. "I can't believe how quickly the year has passed."

"Time does march on; it waits for no man—and even when it isn't always good times," Liz commented.

"Days do come and go," Megan offered her sentiments in a melancholy tone.

"Well," Emma stated, shaking her negative feelings, "I'm ready for the holiday festivities and fun times with friends and family."

The house was decorated beautifully for the Christmas season. Evergreen branches had been pushed into every nook and bookshelf as well as a shaped into a wreath for the front door. Their fragrance filled the porch and rooms, emphasizing the holiday season.

"We still have candy to make and the tree to finish, but we're almost ready," Liz noted as she looked about and checked her list. "I still enjoy celebrating here in town with all of our family and friends!"

"Heath and Anna will come with all of their girls. Samuel and Abby will walk over from Main Street, and Tex should still be in town too." Megan commented after putting another pie in the oven. "I hope it works out for Thomas to bring Blue, John and Chet to town. Surely, the cattle can get along for a day and a half without a cowboy!"

Emma stopped to clean her hands of the sticky, red juice and thought, *It would be good to have some extended time with Chet. Surely, all is well with him by now.* "Yes, I would love to see Chet and the others. It's been so long since we have had a fun, relaxed get-together with everyone—just like it used to be!"

Emma took a deep breath and released it slowly. *Yes, I need to clear things up with my friend. This misunderstanding has gone on way too long. Surely, he isn't still pouting out at the ranch.* Liz hadn't even been back and forth much during the last half of the year. Once she had asked Thomas about Chet, and he answered, "We've been shorthanded, and Chet always chooses to do the extra work."

But everyone would gather that night on Christmas Eve. They would eat, visit, play games, and exchange gifts with the little ones. The next day they would enjoy a Christmas turkey dinner with all the trimmings. The food dishes had been prepared by all of the women, and a real feast was served. The Christmas story of the birth of Jesus would be read by Pastor Parker from his worn pages, and then Anna would start some Christmas carols.

The door swung open, startling the women and little girls. Mattie spun around and leaped with joy as Tex held up a big turkey.

"Oh, Tex, it's just a lovely bird and a perfect size for everyone! Thank you!" Liz took the heavy bird to the work area of the kitchen. Tex tousled the little girls' curls. Mattie squealed with delight. Then he scooped up big-eyed Sofie, "Hey, little ones, are you ready for Santa? He rides in to visit in just a few hours."

"Really?" Mattie squealed with excitement and put her arms around Tex's neck. She rubbed his white, whiskery stubble and placed a kiss on his cheek. "Why, Tex? Why have you been gone so long? Don't you know we miss you?"

Liz thought Tex would melt, but he kept it together as he swung both girls in the air.

"Have you seen Luke?" Mattie asked. "I want him to come home for Christmas too."

"No, I'm sorry," Tex paused and set them down on the bench at the table. "He has some really important work of getting the news to California."

"Go ahead and stay, Tex." Liz placed a hot mug of coffee in front of him. Then Emma put a slice of pecan pie on the table.

"Oh, you women are gonna fatten me up more than that ol' Tom Turkey over there." Tex put his fork in the crust for a big bite. "You know, it's gonna be good with the crust that perfect color. Only one other woman I knew could make crust like that."

Megan stopped and wondered if he was speaking of his wife of long ago. He never mentioned his family that he no longer had, and she could only remember one time when he had spoken of them. *I'm happy that our friend has chosen to spend this holiday with us.*

"Liz, you know, it was a good cotton crop this year," Tex stated as he ate his pie. "If anyone needs or wants a new cotton-filled mattress for his bed, that woman who does laundry can make them. I saw her this week when she did some laundry for me. It would be nice to help her out some. I learned her husband was shot at one of the gambling halls a few weeks ago. I think she has one little girl. Her older son stayed with the wagon train they had traveled with. He was old enough to work and hired on with a family."

Liz sat across the table and listened. "I will," she said, concerned. "We could use one at the ranch, and I'll spread the word at the Mercantile too."

The girls were busy at the tree, putting on the last ornaments that they had made. Liz took the opportunity to talk with Tex. "What do you really think about this talk of war?" she asked quietly.

A little surprised at her question, Tex looked at Liz. "You want to know what I really think?"

She shook her head yes. "Tex, I need to be prepared."

"We have three million slaves in the South and six million other citizens. Most aren't slave owners—just hard working people like you and your family." Tex took a sip of the hot coffee and rested his fork. "Ol' Eli didn't have a clue that the cotton gin he made would increase the slave labor like it has. We went from a hundred bales a week to a thousand or more bales. That machine made that white, fluffy stuff turn into white gold. It's been a steady progression to where we are today, and I, for one, am ready to get it settled. America can't be all it could be until this issue is settled. I do think Lincoln is the man to do it. We have only one gunpowder factory in the South, no gun factory and only thirty percent of the railroad tracks. Hopefully, it will be a short fight, and we can get on to being great again and put this issue of owning a man behind us."

He paused again, took a bite, and had another drink of coffee. "We have a job to do, and we will be great at it." Tex then looked at Liz real serious, "I hope all your menfolk come home safe. You know I'm gonna do my best to get them back to all of you."

Liz placed her hand over his. "Thank you, Tex, for telling me straight, and thank you for your promise," she stated sincerely.

"Liz, celebrate real good tonight and tomorrow. We might need to hold on to it for a while."

Nodding her head in understanding, Liz blinked back a tear.

"Okay, Mattie," Tex called out, "get those checkers out. I think I'm gonna beat you!" He snickered as he turned his thoughts and attention to the always-bubbling Mattie.

Liz placed her hand on Tex's shoulder as she stood to go prepare the turkey. Megan heard horses out front and a single wagon pull in, then voices on the steps as everyone started arriving to celebrate on Christmas Eve.

During supper, Emma could feel Chet's eyes on her. She smiled. When she brought the coffeepot to the table and refilled his cup, she leaned closer and quietly said, "Chet, it's pretty nice outside. Let's go out to the porch to talk." He looked up at her invitation and nodded.

It wasn't long till the dishes were clean, and she looked for Chet. She stepped out on the porch, and he came from the barn where he had been checking the horses. "Guess you have been real busy at the ranch, shorthanded and all," Emma started the conversation. "I miss seeing you at the restaurant or on the weekend."

He stepped up on the porch and leaned against a post. "It's been busy, that's all."

"Chet?" she asked as he looked her way. "Let's be honest with each other. I don't think either of us knows what has happened. What changed between us?" She leaned forward in her chair.

Chet was quiet. He swallowed and looked away, thinking back. "It seems so long ago…I'm not sure it really matters anymore." Chet's voice was low as he looked back at Emma with a deep sadness reflecting in his eyes.

Emma felt sorry for her friend. She never meant him any harm or hurt, but she still needed to know what had happened. "I think we need to work this out, Chet. You're my friend, and I can tell you are still upset with me." She paused. "What did I do?"

"Well..." he stammered. "I just thought..." he stopped again. "It's like this." Chet stood up straight and started over again. "I came into town one day during the middle of the week. I was dropping off something at the smithy for Thomas. I was gonna have lunch with you while I waited for Luther to fix it, and I saw you..." Chet stopped mid-sentence.

Emma couldn't imagine what he had seen. She didn't remember any of it. "What exactly did you see?"

"I saw you laughing and talking with a cowboy in front of your place on the boardwalk." Chet was embarrassed to admit the sight had made him jealous. "I don't know what happened; I was surprised by the way I felt. I was angrier and angrier the longer I watched the two of you. I thought...well, I thought you were interested in another person. That's when I realized I had real feelings for you. The longer I stayed away or thought about it...or the more I tried to fix it, the worse it got."

Emma sat silent. She had never known that he had come to town that day. To be truthful, she didn't even remember the cowboy.

"That cowboy was flirting with you, and you liked it! You flirted back." He looked at her with no expression. "Then I came into town to try to talk with you, and I got all upset and tongue-tied. Just blurted out if you wanted to get married, and then you were insulted and said 'No.' I just didn't know what to do or how to fix it."

Emma understood a little better now. "Did you really think I was trying to make you jealous and that I wanted to push the issue of marriage?"

Chet listened and finally said, "I guess...maybe so."

"Chet, you know, I'm a direct woman and don't play those silly games. I didn't even know you were in town, and I don't even remember who I might have been talking with that day. I'm not one of those bargirls up the road at the saloons and gambling halls. I feed the ones who come into the restaurant to get a good meal. I'm friendly, but I don't worry about their coming back or leaving any extra money on the table. They only have to come in once to know that about me. If they get out of line, they leave hungry, and they don't want that!"

Chet scuffed a boot on the wooden planks of the porch and went down a step or two, thinking. He knew Emma was right.

Emma stood and went to the porch post where Chet had been standing. "I'm sorry I hurt your feelings hurt, Chet. I never meant to. The day you came and asked if I wanted to get married...well, I was so shocked. I didn't think you were serious. I didn't know where you were coming from. Can't we just go back to the way it was?" Emma inquired.

Chet turned on the step to look Emma in the face. "All this time away from you I've tried to forget you, Emma, but I can't. I realized I love you, and I don't want you being friendly with other cowboys. I've fought it. I know you aren't gonna change, and that's part of why I love you. You are straightforward and spunky and confident. You don't need a man like other women do. But I want a woman who does want me, and it's obvious you don't. So, no! I can't go back to the way it was. I live in a bunkhouse with a bunch of other dirty cowboys. I have no place to put you even if you did want me; and no, I'm not gonna live in the Mailly house with you, Megan, Jackson and Lydia. I'm not gonna be a man who lives in a house provided by a woman!"

Emma backed away and looked at Chet. He was upset and angry again. "I'm sorry about that. At least, I know now what's on your mind. I'm not sure at the moment if you love me or hate me, but I'm pretty sure going back to our friendship the way it was isn't going to happen."

Still upset, Chet said, "And I've thought about who that bunkhouse belongs to on the Rolling M. It's Thomas'—not Liz Mailly's!"

With everything said, Chet looked into Emma's emerald-green eyes and decided to kiss her—upset or not! *I might never have another chance.* He placed his hands on Emma's cheeks and gently, purposefully, kissed her—a long kiss that she wouldn't easily forget. For some reason, Emma didn't move or wiggle away but allowed him to kiss her thoroughly.

Holding her and still close to her face, Chet softly said, "I love you, Emma, and no, we can't go back to just being friends."

Emma stared at him and listened, still numb from his kiss.

"Merry Christmas, Em." Chet dropped his hands and stepped back, taking two steps at a time. He didn't look back as he walked to the barn where his saddled horse waited.

Emma remained on the porch until she could no longer see Chet riding away. Deep in thought, she was startled when Liz came to the door. "Emma, we are about to open gifts and read the Christmas story. Come on in, honey, and warm up by the fire."

Chapter 25

Late Winter 1861

Chet hadn't seen Emma since their Christmas Eve conversation. He had spent the last several weeks thinking about their talk. Over and over he rolled it around in his head till he had worn it out. Every pony in the stables knew about Emma. Chet had talked it out with all of them. They would twitch their ears and, maybe, neigh with a toss of their head when he got riled up some. He knew that he loved her, and now that he had admitted his feelings, the love continued to grow even if Emma didn't water it any.

Chet had been in town at least once a week since then, but he never went to Emma's Table to eat or talk with her. Until he had a plan on how to handle the situation, he wouldn't go. He simply watched her from afar each time. She was still her feisty self, but he didn't see her linger with any one person. In fact, Chet mostly saw her with the two little girls of Liz and Thomas. He laughed, thinking on how Mattie kept both the door of the Mercantile and Emma's Table swinging. In and out, she went a dozen times a day.

On Monday, Mattie had Emma coming and going with her. He saw Emma a little more on that day. The weather was a little nippy, and Emma's cheeks grew rosy with the cold. She looked so pretty in her dark-green dress that matched her emerald-green eyes. Her dark curls were fixed in a style that was long down her back and pulled back on the sides. Emma had matured into a lovely, young woman—no longer the sullen, dark girl he had met on the wagon trail. He really hadn't paid much attention to her at all five years ago.

Chet wasn't sure when he fell in love with her, but he was facing the most frustrating time in his life. He played the picture of her on that day over and over in his mind.

Thomas came into the barn where Chet was currying down the workhorses of the day. Chet nodded at Thomas and grabbed a different brush for the mane. He liked his horses to look and feel good.

"How did things go today?" Thomas asked.

"Good. Brought all of the horses in the pasture close to the house."

"Ya," Thomas replied. "I saw them; they look good."

"I had time so I went to look over the cattle. It won't be much work to bring them in closer tomorrow. Even with John and Blue working as freight hands this week for Liz, we should be able to get it done quickly." Chet continued brushing as he talked over the workload with his boss.

Thomas nodded his head in agreement. He lingered and was quiet, waiting to see if his friend needed to talk some more. Liz had pushed him some, trying to see how Chet and Emma were. Emma had kept her silence with the women, and Chet had been silent with the men. Everyone kept going about work as normal, when all the while everyone knew Chet loved Emma—even little Mattie.

"Everything okay, Thomas?" Chet looked over the top of the horse. "I mean everything other than the politics on all of our minds." He chuckled a little, knowing what he had said was silly as the matter of secession weighed heavily on every adult south of the Mason-Dixon Line.

"I was just wondering how you and Emma are or how you two left things…" Thomas paused. "I haven't seen you with her since Christmas, and then you didn't seem to stay long."

Chet stopped brushing the animal and listened to Thomas, deciding the time had come to talk about the matter with his friend. "It's been a long and painful process. I've even thought about you and Miss Liz and how long you waited for her. She even pushed you away too." Chet had gained a little courage from that observation. "I don't know how you could do that, Thomas!" Chet exclaimed.

Thomas could hear the pain in Chet's voice and thought back to his years of waiting. "I knew I loved her and had to convince her to love me back. Once we worked it out, it's been the best years of my life."

"What do I do, Thomas? How do I convince her?" Chet came around the horse to sit on a hay bale. He realized he desperately needed to talk about his love for Emma to someone other than a four-footed, furry one.

"I'm convinced you can get any woman to love you if you love her first. We are to love our wives like Christ loves the church. **God loved us first.** That persistent, kind, patient—always there—kind of love."

Chet listened and thought before he replied, "But I'm not always there."

"Maybe not, but you can always be on her mind and let her know you aren't far away. Go and talk with her like normal—like it used to be—just fun stuff and nothing serious. I know she misses that, Chet. She told Liz she did."

Chet's head jerked up as he looked at Thomas. "She did?"

"She didn't say this exactly, but I think she has really missed you, Chet."

"Well, maybe..." Chet felt hopeful. "Like Christ..." Chet repeated out loud. "Thomas, I'm not much like Christ."

Thomas laughed, "None of us are, buddy, but would you lay down your life for Emma?"

"Sure," Chet said, not even having to think.

"That's pretty Christ-like—to lay down your life for another, isn't it, Chet?"

"Those Mailly women are pretty tough cookies. I'm not sure any of them needs a man."

Thomas laughed, "Yes, they are, but think about it…a meek woman wouldn't last long out here. Don't let them fool you. Emma needs you in the best way—not to feed and clothe her—but to love her. You simply have to look at it in a different way than most men do. Don't get caught up in always doing things for her, but in how to love her, how to feed her heart and her mind. That keeps her close to you and waiting every minute till she sees you again. Stay patient and be calm; ask God to help you find ways and keep your emotions from getting riled up and frustrated."

Chet slowly nodded, understanding and thinking. "Okay, Thomas, so you think I should try to go at this again and not give up and try to stay away?"

"If you really love her, Chet, it will never go away. Remember how many years I longed for Liz?"

Chet's head jerked up. "Oh, I could never do that."

"Then get at it, Chet. Start making a love story!" Thomas slapped Chet on the back and turned to leave.

Over the next several days Chet started writing letters, just short letters. He wrote little notes of what was on his mind and what he thought about when it came to Miss Emma.

❀ ❀ ❀

Chet leaped on his horse with his pocket full of notes. Lulu announced she was out of coffee, and Chet quickly volunteered to make a run into town. With every turn of the dirt road, he pondered what to say when he saw Emma. Chet stopped at the edge of town on Hell's Avenue. He thought about a shot of whiskey to calm his nerves and warm up a bit; the winter day had a chill to it. Instead, he voiced a prayer of encouragement, remounted his horse and quickly galloped to Luther's Livery.

"Hey, Chet, haven't seen you in a whole set of days. What can I do for you?"

"Well, I need the back shoes checked on this pony. I think she has a sore foot. Lulu needs coffee, so I need to go get that too."

"Sure thing," Luther said, "might be a while."

"No problem. I'll be catching a cup of coffee and a dessert over at Emma's," Chet said so calmly and normal that Luther was surprised. Luther looked up quickly from examining the pony's foot, "You goin' down to Emma's?"

"Yeah, that okay?"

"Sure…sure thing, Mr. Chet. A man's got to eat, and that girl can cook. Guess everyone makes it her way time and time again." He began examining the horse's shoe.

Chet watched Luther, a little confused over his inquiry about his going to eat at Emma's. He finally turned and headed down the dirt road and up the steps at Liz's store. The door jingled, and Liz looked up to see him. "Hi, Miss Liz."

"Hello, Chet," she looked behind Chet to see if he were alone.

"Lulu needs coffee, and my horse is getting a shoe checked. I'll be back in a while to get the coffee. I'm going to wait it out at Emma's." Chet was as calm as could be when he talked—like waiting at Emma's was a commonplace thing to do.

Liz's eyes were big as she blinked, trying to sort out what Chet was saying. "Oh," she paused, "you are going over to Emma's?"

"Ya, I'll be back for the coffee in a while." Chet turned with a smile and went out Liz's door. He walked a few steps to Emma's and pushed open her door.

Threads of Courage

❖ ❖ ❖

"I'll be right with you," Emma called out. She had her back turned and didn't know who had come into the restaurant. She pulled the last bit of chocolate icing across the chocolate cake.

Chet walked closer and watched her place huge pecan halves in rows on the cake. She then put a sheet of cookies in the oven. Emma was drying her hands as she turned to care for her customer's needs. Chet was a quite close now. Her eyes took in his chest then quickly travelled up to Chet's eyes. She was taken by surprise, but Chet let no vibes off that he was. In fact, he was cool and calm.

Chet stepped back, pulled his arms from his sheepskin coat, brushed his long hair from his face and sat down. Emma watched, unaware she wasn't working or talking. She finally stuttered, "Would… would you like some coffee?"

"Thank you, Emma, I would. It's right cold out today. I got chilled riding into town. Hope Ol' Man Winter isn't going to make one last appearance."

Emma stepped over to get a hot drink, turning her back to him to calm herself. She slowly regained her composure. "Would you like some chocolate cake too?" she asked. *Does my voice sound normal?*

"If it's that one you just put those big pecans on, I sure do! Make it a big slice. It's been ages since I've enjoyed some of your cooking. I was hoping that I had timed it just right."

Emma slowly turned toward him. *Just what has gotten into him,* she wondered. "Sure, Chet, I'll cut you a double slice." Bringing the cake to him, she eyed him with more composure.

Watching as Emma set the plate in front of him, Chet patted the table, and asked, "Got time to sit with me a while? Your cookies aren't ready yet."

Emma locked eyes with Chet.

"Em, please sit with me for a minute."

Pulling out the chair, Emma slowly sat down.

Calmly, Chet pushed his fork into the warm cake and cut off a good-sized bite, putting it in his mouth, savoring the taste and smiling with delight. "You still got it, Em. You know, Lulu is a right good cook, but once you've tasted the food at Emma's Table, nothing compares."

Emma sat properly across the table—speechless at his glowing compliments!

"So Emma, what's been going on in town? Much action this chillin' time of year?" He took another bite and a drink of coffee.

Emma relaxed some. "No, pretty quiet," she drew the words out.

Chet talked and carried the conversation. She got up to take out the cookies and put another tray into the hot oven. He told her about the horse and the new calves. About Callie the cat with nine lives and one crooked ear. He didn't mention war, politics or their past uncomfortable encounters. Emma thought, *It's as if they never happened!* She stopped to sit at the table with him, and they laughed together. By the end of the afternoon, she had shared some funny stories of things that had happened in town.

Luther showed up at the door to inform Chet that his horse was ready. "Mr. Chet?" he looked around.

When Chet called, "Hey, Luther, come in. I'll buy you a piece of Emma's cake," the blacksmith looked suspiciously from one to the other.

"Sure, Luther, come on in," Emma said with more joy in her heart than she had felt in months.

Chet smiled. Seeing Emma's delight, he felt real joy, too—not just the kind he had to push up over the past.

"Well, glory be!" Luther said as he sat down with Chet and

Emma. *What an unusual group of friends,* Luther thought. "Miss Emma, you're happy today?"

"Yes, Mr. Wheeler, I am!" she smiled and placed his cake in front of him.

"How is that horse?" Chet asked.

"She's good. The shoe needed to have a little work. Her hoof might be tender, stone-bruised from the pebble that was lodged in it. If you want to take my horse and let the mare rest a day or so, I'll take good care of her. Might even use some of Miss Emma's lavender she loves so much. It seems to be good on most anything—man or beast. Miss Emma," Luther asked, "how did you know about that? I only knew an old slave in Mississippi who could brew that up like you do."

"Really?" Emma asked. "I learned it from an old slave at my daddy's plantation in Mississippi."

Luther sat up straighter. "Your pappy had slaves and a plantation in Mississippi?"

"Yes," Emma answered, thinking maybe she shouldn't have answered so readily. "Close to Vicksburg," she said slowly. "Two were my good friends, and I hated to leave them behind. Isaac took care of our horses, and I learned so much from him. Papa didn't like my visiting the stables, but I loved horses so much that I would sneak off and go there."

Luther listened, letting her talk. *Maybe I could learn more from her...* He tried to remove all evidence of the shocked look he had displayed earlier at her unexpected announcement.

"Then my housemaid Nellie was close to my age. I want to try to get her here with me. I miss Nellie." Emma grew quiet as she thought about her friend.

Chet had also learned some things he hadn't known about

Emma. He didn't know much of anything about her life in Mississippi, except she wasn't fond of her parents, especially her father.

Before Chet left for home, riding one of Luther's horses, he decided to leave one note for Emma by her flour bin. Since he would have to return Luther's horse, he decided to take the others back to the ranch with him. Even though his mind was elsewhere, he didn't forget the coffee for Miss Lulu.

Chapter 26

Emma couldn't sleep again, so she rose and dressed for the day and then tiptoed out of her room. She laced up her black boots by the light of the kitchen lamp. "Might as well go start the kitchen routine at the restaurant," she quietly said out loud as she took a deep breath and yawned. She knew she needed to prepare a new batch of cinnamon rolls. The day before the cowboys had wiped her clean out of everything.

When she reached the restaurant, she decided to start the bread first and reached into her flour bin to scoop the white powder into her bowl. A letter dropped to the floor. She picked it up, having no clue who put it there or how. She opened the note and read.

Good morning, Emma,

I sure enjoyed your dessert and our conversation this afternoon. I'll be back in to pick up the horse at Luther's in a day or so. If the weather holds, I'll be back in for church Sunday. I haven't heard Parker preach in a good while, and I need to see that new baby girl, Aubrey Faith.

I hope you have a good day.

Your friend,

Chet

Emma was very surprised to receive a note from the cowboy.

Then she noticed his note had brought a huge smile to her face. *When did he write this note?* she wondered. *How did he manage to place it here where I would find it later?*

The door pushed open, and she saw Luther arrive for breakfast. "Hi, Miss Emma, I saw the light on early and came on in. If you aren't ready for my breakfast, just give me a cup of coffee, and I'll wait over here. Miss Liz let me borrow a paper last evening." Luther pulled out a chair to sit and read. "You're happy this early morn."

Emma tried to smile smaller but couldn't. She slipped the note in her apron pocket. "Sure, I'll get your coffee. Let me get this bread rising, and then I'll get your breakfast." She kneaded the bread and thought about Luther reading. She really didn't know much about his past and whether or not he had ever been a slave.

Bringing his breakfast over to him, Emma asked if she could sit with him. She always asked, and he always said, "Yes, for a few minutes, ma'am."

"Can I ask you a few questions about yourself?" she asked that day, not knowing how he would respond.

He looked up in surprise. "I suppose."

"How or when did you learn to read?"

"The mistress at the plantation wanted us to learn to read the Bible. We had a little, broken-down, cold cabin that served as our church. She gave us Sunday as a day of rest. She cared for our illnesses when we were under the weather. She had a mammy that she had taught to read at the big house, and that woman taught us little ones to read on Sunday."

"Were you born on the plantation?" Emma sat, thinking about Luther's life and how lonely it could be.

"Yes, I lived in Mississippi."

"I'll get you some more coffee," she said as she watched him drink to the bottom of the cup. "How were you freed?" she asked as she poured the hot liquid into his cup.

Luther took a sip. "My name is Wheeler. I worked as a young boy in the repairs at the plantation wagon house. I was a good smithy and wheel master. So my given name became Luther Wheeler." He leaned back in the chair, thinking of years gone by. "One day the Master's little boy came playing around where we were building new wheels. We warned him that it was dangerous, and he should move along. He was climbing above us, lost his footing and fell into the area where we were working around a forge. When he fell, he knocked a pot of molten metal on some other slaves who were working. Instead of helping my coworkers, I caught him as he fell. My friends were badly burned, and one died from his injuries. Because I saved the young master, his mother insisted that I be freed—as payment for saving his life. Her insistence that I be freed brought her much grief, but I was freed."

Emma thought he looked sad. "You saved the boy? Being given your freedom was good, right?"

"Not really. Everything I loved and needed was there—my home, my family. Then I had to leave and make it on my own in a world that didn't accept free black men."

Emma sat, thinking about what he had said. *I have never thought about slavery in this way.* She rose to get his lunch that she packed each morning.

"Emma," Luther said.

She returned with his lunch in a bag.

"Remember how we talked about God?"

She nodded, "Yes."

"I was in bondage at that plantation—held captive by the only life I knew. When I was given my freedom, I had to trust and go with it. You are held in bondage by your sin and your lack of trust in God. Freedom and a new life is waiting. You just gotta go with it."

Emma knew that Luther and Pastor Parker were right. She needed to give God a chance and trust in Him.

Chapter 27

Liz was waiting for the freight wagons to arrive any day. She had placed one of her largest orders ever, anticipating the interruption of supplies or even the non-availability of items. She had taken Tex's words of warning to heart and planned ahead as best she knew how. Liz had even taken John and Blue away from the ranch for the week to help with getting all of her freight and multiple wagon loads of goods.

Liz had been forced to hire some men she didn't know to help with the freight supply wagons. Over the past few months, she'd had very little available labor at her fingertips. Liz wasn't happy using these workmen but felt she had no other choice. Thomas justified her decision by saying that strangers had pulled her freight to the point where her men picked up the load. "It really isn't any different doing it this way," he had said.

On the last two shipments, Liz had noticed the wagons had extra room. She thought her wagons would be completely full and would have ordered more supplies if she had known. She stopped for a moment, looking at her freight ledger. Confused, Liz flipped a few pages back and forth.

Abby sat in the rocker at the back of the Mercantile, sewing while Liz worked on her ledgers. She noticed Liz's frustration and heard her sigh. "What is it, Liz?"

"I'm not sure. I can't put my finger on it, but it doesn't add up." Liz turned another page with additional numbers and notes.

"Like what? What are you thinking?" Abby thought if Liz spoke it, maybe what didn't add up would become clear to her.

"I'm behind in my freight bookkeeping—my first mistake," she admitted. "Now I can't make sense of it all. You know," she continued, talking to her schoolteacher cousin. "I have been ordering more than usual for several months, stockpiling supplies for troubled times."

Abby nodded, and she held the sewing in her hand as she gave her full attention to Liz's explanation.

"First, I had lots of back orders, which would make more room in the wagon's wasted space. My drivers say that the wagons were full, but when they arrived they had extra space. It just doesn't add up, and it's multiple shipments—not just one mishap or one freight load."

"Hmmm," Abby tilted her head to the left, "what do John and Blue say or Chet?"

"They haven't been on all the runs because Thomas has been shorthanded, and it's calving season," Liz stopped to face Abby. "With multiple new drivers, I can't get any one story or information from them. But I know something is definitely wrong."

"I'm not sure I understand…"

Liz was puzzled. "I'm not sure I do either."

"Just give me your thoughts in a fact statement," Abby stated. "Maybe it will help."

Liz paused. "I'm not getting all that I ordered." She held up one finger. "Two…" she raised two fingers. "…the wagons have room for more when they arrive here." She paused again, thinking, and raised a third finger. "Three, they say the wagon is full and won't ship previously delayed items; and, fourth, at some point, the drivers tell me they are full."

"But they aren't full when they get here?" Abby asked, trying to be a help.

"No-o-o-o," Liz stretched out her reply, thinking. "John and Chet are gone now with Blue to get this last big load. The wagons are full with lots of orders. I hope they can shed some light on what has been happening."

Emma came around from the other side of the room where she had been doing her own bookwork. She had to separate the egg bill she had received from Liz and deduct it from the flour, sugar and spices she needed for her restaurant. Because Liz sold so many eggs for Emma as well as some little chicks, Emma seldom had to put out any money against her bill with the Mercantile.

"Liz, I've got mine completed. Do you want to double-check it for me?" Emma smiled at Abby as Liz was still in deep thought over her freight-wagon dilemma.

"Hi, Emma! Did you see your letter on the counter? That's two this week. Do you have a new pen pal?" Abby raised her eyebrow as she teased her sister about the recent letters.

"Oh, thank you," Emma said as she walked back to look for it without answering her sister.

The first letter was a nice, short, one-page note from Chet. Emma had been surprised when she opened and read it. She had read it several times over the last few days.

The handwriting on the envelope told her that Chet was also the writer of this one. Slipping it into her apron pocket, Emma bid her sister and Liz goodbye as she quietly returned to her business next door. When she saw that the restaurant was empty, she took a moment to read the note.

She reached in an empty tin on her shelf and pulled out the other two letters. She took the envelope from her pocket, open it, slipped out the enclosed letter and read:

> Hi Em,
>
> I thought about that chocolate cake again today. I circled the herd of cattle twice I was so lost in thought. I'm glad you took time to sit with me that day. I have missed your voice and your friendship. Things just go better and look better with you around.
> Luther got the horse fixed up, and I made it back in quick time the following day. Sorry, I didn't have time to come down the street for more of your cooking.
> Hope you have a really good day.
>
> Your friend,
>
> Chet

She read the letter over again, pausing at the beginning—*Hi Em.* Only Chet and Mattie called her "Em." She like it and read his note again.

With anticipation, Emma picked up the new letter she had received that day. *It's only been a few days since I received the last letter.* A sense of excitement gripped her as she opened it and read his words.

> Hi Em,
>
> Real sorry I didn't get to see you before I left with Blue and John for the freight wagon pickup. We would have loved to have you pack us some food for the trail, but Lulu did a good job on the food for us. I'm sure you know Liz has a big order of supplies coming in, and she needed three drivers—one for each wagon. They are to be big loads with these real pretty workhorses pulling them. These horses have the feathering at

the ankles like their manes. I remember seeing these horses when we were in Louisiana all those years ago.

Was thinking the other day and wondered where all the time went. When we were in those wagons headed West, I thought you were sweet on Ranger Colt and he on you. Then he went on to Birdville to be the sheriff. We don't see him much over the years. Always liked Colt and counted him as my friend. I'm sure you do too.

We'll ride two days, meet Liz's wagons, tie our horses to the back of them and head back to Fort Worth. I'm sure we will be hungry as a pack of wolves. We'll stop in to eat. Make sure you got plenty for us.

Your friend,

Chet

She thoughtfully traced his last three words with her finger.

Emma knew pretty much all he had shared, but she enjoyed receiving the letter. She could hear Chet's voice with his cadence on each sentence. She stood and put all three letters in the empty tin, replaced down the lid, and slid it to the back of the shelf. She never knew how much she would enjoy a letter from Chet.

Three days had passed and the freight was due at the Mercantile. Liz paced the wooden sidewalk out front and looked in both directions. Cowboys went one way toward Hell's Avenue, and school kids walked the other way. No freight wagons yet for her. She didn't know why the load's delivery made her so on edge.

❦ ❦ ❦

A few miles out of town, a wagon sat parked under a group of oak trees. The sun was shining, the breeze light, and as far as a Texas winter day goes, it couldn't get much better. A creek was close, and the men watered their horses while they rested and waited.

"Did Mr. Barton say how much this time?"

"No, he didn't—just said it was a double load of whiskey and some good bourbon too."

"Do we get money this time for the load or did you trade for whiskey again?"

"We get both. It's a double load."

"Hmmm."

The men talked back and forth and then stood when they saw the three wagons coming down the road.

Chet motioned to the other two freight wagons to pull over and water the horses before they went the last few miles into Fort Worth. John pulled in on one side of Chet with Blue coming in on the other. The two men in the empty wagon looked them over. "Those are different drivers," one said to the other.

"Pay it no mind. Mr. Barton didn't give us any warning on any difference. They pulled in, so must be the same deal."

"Howdy," the bigger man said, walking a few steps over to Liz's wagons. "You got our freight like usual?"

Chet looked at Blue and John. They both shrugged, not knowing anything. "I'm not sure what you mean, sir," Chet replied.

"Ya, like always, you know. We are here to pick up the load."

"What load would that be?" Chet asked again. "All of this is for Liz at the Mercantile."

"Ya, she knows all about it. Got it worked out with our boss 'cause if, well, you know, the nature of the shipment."

"Who is your boss?" Chet asked.

"Mr. Barton, you know him? He owns most of the businesses and buildings down on Hell's Avenue in Fort Worth."

Chet nodded, "Oh, and the nature of goods is whiskey?"

"Ya, you got it. Mr. Barton didn't want that lady at the Mercantile embarrassed and all. He worked out a special deal with her."

John and Blue looked at Chet. All three had figured out this "deal" fairly quickly. Liz would never supply the saloons and gambling halls with these spirits. Chet worked on a plan in his head. He didn't want any trouble with these guys, knowing they wouldn't be easy to take.

"Well, you know, Miss Liz is waiting to get her supply in quickly today, and your load is loaded down front at the bottom. It would take too long to do it here. Why don't you take a nap in the warm sunshine? We will get this unloaded at Liz's and then run those boxes down to you and your boss. You said Mr. Barton, right?"

The two men looked at each other. "Well, we would need to get paid and all," the man said, thinking about Chet's offer.

"No problem," Chet pulled a coin from his vest pocket and flipped it to the man. The man caught the shiny gold coin sparkling in the sunlight. "We got whiskey coming too."

"No problem either," Chet replied, smiling. "Liz will make sure you and your boss will get what's coming to you."

"Okay, then, it's a deal," the man smiled broadly—like he had made the best deal in the world.

The other man said to his partner, "So we get paid and don't have to do the work?"

"Yep," the deal-maker replied. "Now don't forget to show up at the Mercantile. We want to make sure you get the end of the deal."

John had to turn away. He was about to laugh out loud.

Blue joined in sealing the deal. "Ya, we will catch you later."

Both men pulled their hats down for a quick afternoon nap.

Chet took the teams at a fast pace the rest of the way into town.

In front of the Mercantile, he pulled the horses up quick. "You guys hurry in to tell Liz. I'm lookin' up Sheriff Jackson."

※ ※ ※

"You've got to be kidding me," Liz said, her hands on her hips as she listened.

"Jackson's coming now?" she asked.

"Ya, Chet's looking for him."

Chet saw Jackson coming down the road from the other side of town—the side Barton owned. He jogged up to him and waved him over. Jackson listened intently to the story and looked back to Hell's Avenue.

"Have you looked in the wagon to see if the load is there?" Jackson asked.

"No, not yet. We hurried on into town to tell you and Liz," Chet replied with each step as the two marched to the Mercantile.

"I should have known!" Liz paced three or four steps then turned around again. "Let's take the wagon to the back to unload and get the proof."

The men took the wagons around back and, before long, found the tarp covering the whiskey.

"Look," Liz pointed, "the boxes even have his name on them."

"That's even better proof," Jackson smiled.

"You boys are hereby my deputies for the rest of the day. Guard these and arrest the other two men when they show up to be paid. I'm going down to pay Barton a visit," Jackson barked out orders, tossing three badges to his friends.

Liz stood at her front windows until she saw Barton being escorted into the new jail. When he looked toward her, his handsome face contorted in ugly rage. Within the hour, the other two men were marched into the jail by Liz's friends.

Jackson came into the Mercantile at closing. "They aren't saying much but denying most of it. The name on his shipment is pretty good evidence against him. If it had your name on them, I would have to let them all walk. I'll hold them overnight. Liz, you need to decide what you want to do about it. I know you don't want money. I can't hang them over this like it was stealing livestock. So not much I can do except keep them in jail a few days."

"Thank you," Liz said. "I'll have an answer in the morning."

The next morning Jackson came over to see what Liz had decided. "Can you keep them a few days and make them pay a tax or fine? Can you keep the fine money for the town? We can use it on some community project or something," she paused. "I hate that he wanted to give to charity for the freight in the beginning, and I refused. He got his way." Liz was furious with that thought. She didn't want Barton to win.

"Okay, Liz, we can do that," Jackson agreed.

Chapter 28

Spring 1861

It wasn't long before the political problems the women tried not to talk or think about happened as well as what the whole state or nation expected. In January, South Carolina was the first state to draft the official papers of seceding. In a matter of days, Mississippi, Florida, Alabama, Georgia, Louisiana, and finally, Texas seceded and formed the Confederate States of America. A meeting in Montgomery, Alabama, bound the states together with a new constitution much like the Union's but with greater emphasis on the autonomy of each state. Jefferson Davis was named President until an election could be organized.

Liz opened the most current newspaper in the store and read the March 4, 1861, St. Louis paper. The banner headline read: LINCOLN'S INAUGURATION. "The new president has no plans to end slavery in the states where it already exists," Liz read out loud to Megan and paused before she read the next line.

Megan leaned over her sister's shoulder, trying to get a look for herself, but Lydia, now a year old and walking, squirmed, and Megan couldn't see it. "What else does it say?" she asked, feeling a little anxiety.

"Basically, he won't accept the secession papers from the newly-formed Confederacy and hopes to resolve the national crisis without warfare." Liz sighed as she set the paper down. "I hope so! Oh, I hope so! I have worried and fretted over this. I've tried to give the whole matter to God, but I keep taking it back."

Threads of Courage

"What about Fort Sumter in South Carolina?" Megan asked as she bounced Lydia and tried to get her to sleep. Lydia was plump and pink, a pretty little girl with big blue eyes and just a short crop of shiny blonde curls. A soft wisp of curls framed her face, giving her the sweetest cherubic look.

"It's a tangled mess as usual. In a previous paper, President Buchanan refused to surrender any Southern forts to the seceding states, so Southern troops seized them. He is leaving office, and Lincoln wasn't quite there yet. One hand doesn't know what the other is doing."

"So we have Southern troops already?" Megan was surprised. She quickly tried to think if Jackson had given her any information on this. She knew he would be quick to join, and she mentally tried to prepare herself for this decision.

"Yes, I guess so," Liz replied. "At Fort Sumter, the Southern troops pushed the Union supply ship back and wouldn't let it resupply the fort. The ship returned to New York with the undeliverable goods. General Beauregard demanded the fort to surrender to the South before midnight." Then Liz pulled a poster from under her counter. "I've been requested to display this poster." As she turned the poster so Megan could get a full view, her face reflected her sadness.

Megan read the poster, which requested men aged 18 to 40 to sign up for the new Confederate Army.

"I don't know how long I can keep from nailing it up. No one knows I have it yet." Liz and Megan's faces registered the seriousness of what they were facing as well as the rest of the families in the state of Texas and throughout the nation.

"Does the paper give us any glimmer of hope?" Megan asked again as they scanned the words on the newspaper page. Another headline read: "George Williamson Addresses the Texas Secession Convention," and another said "The Confederate Constitution."

"Well, here it is in black and white. You can read as many papers as you wish." Liz patted the stack of winter papers from other areas. Every paper North or South basically reported the same news. "I think shots will be fired before it's all over. How bad or how long… only time will tell."

"When will you put up the poster for soldiers to enlist?" asked Megan. Her thoughts still haunted her.

"Not until I have to," Liz said and looked out the window of her mercantile. "But it might be sooner than we think."

The two sisters saw their husbands under the roof of the boardwalk in front of Samuel's office. They looked serious as they talked for several minutes.

"Oh, don't worry. I see them talk every day, and every conversation is serious," Megan said, consoling herself as well as her sister. No one has much laughter this winter—just talk of secession and rumors of war. Now with Jackson as the sheriff and in town every day, he and Samuel spend much time together."

"How are you with that?" Liz asked Megan, knowing she didn't want him to take the job but liked having him live in town and not out at the ranch.

"I love having him in my daily life. I don't like the thought of the other so much; at least Main Street and over the hill hasn't presented too much trouble yet. Mostly, the cowboys are tired and hungry. They have to move on pretty quickly. The herd bosses don't let them linger too much. Just knowing that the city now has a lawman has settled them down some."

"You know the lady who does laundry? I think they came from the wagon train over a year ago," Liz mentioned.

"Yes," Megan said, "she has a daughter named Sally. Abby said she is one of her students—a smart girl."

Liz nodded in agreement with her sister. "Tex told me back at Christmas that her husband was shot in one of the gambling halls."

"Maybe just as well," Megan said. "I think he beat her and drank away the little bit of money they had. But I still feel sorry for her; it can't be easy."

"I know," Liz replied. "Hers is a sad story. I did get some mattresses sold for her. I hope it helped some."

❊ ❊ ❊

Samuel and Jackson made their way across the street and up the steps to the red doors of Liz's Mercantile. Samuel looked at both women and nodded "Hello."

"Liz, have you received a government poster?"

Megan looked at Liz to see what she would say.

"Y…yes," she stammered, "I receive official mail often. What are you looking for?"

Jackson spoke up next. "Lt. Colonel Robert E. Lee is removing his 2nd Cavalry troop from Texas and going east to the Confederacy to manage the War Department for President Davis. He has issued posters to be displayed in the towns to start an enlistment for Cavalry troops and foot soldiers."

Liz placed the posters on the counter and stood very somber, thinking for a moment and then asked a question. "Wasn't Jefferson Davis the head of the War Department for the Union and General Lee, the head of West Point, our military academy?"

"Yes, they were." Jackson smiled with pride. "With them heading up this conflict, the North better think twice before battling with the Confederacy. Lee and Davis are good friends, and both have military minds. I believe they might be the best there is. With these two in charge, this should be a quick rebuttal. Lincoln will see it our way right soon," Jackson stated with confidence.

"Thank you," Samuel said as he looked them over. "Put one up in here, and we will post the rest up around town. Here are the official enlistment papers. They can get them from you, Jackson or me. I'll have the master list at my office. No uniforms as of yet, but they are coming. Any questions the soldiers have—send them over to me or Jackson."

Jackson came around the counter to hug Megan and kiss the sleeping Lydia in her arms. He then followed Samuel out the door.

Samuel looked back at Liz and nodded at her, trying to reassure her that he had no control over putting up the posters around town. The bell on the door jingled as he and Jackson walked out with a hammer and nails in their hands.

❀ ❀ ❀

Luke loved riding for the Pony Express. With the election of President Abraham Lincoln, the secession of the Southern states and the birth of the Confederacy, the news he carried West was of monumental importance.

Today as he pushed his pony past magnificent views of snow-capped mountains and lush, spring-green valleys fed by the nutrients of the snow melting in the warmth of the spring sun, Luke felt more alive and grateful than ever before. Whether he was maturing from being on his own in God's glorious creation or from understanding the magnitude of the Union's ripping apart, he didn't know. But he would never be that naïve boy again who began riding a year ago for the overland Pony Express. He understood what was in his mochila. Who knows what would happen when California received the news of the Inaugural Address, the state of the Union with more states seceding each passing day, and the standoff at Fort Sumter, South Carolina. A call had been extended to California to join the Union's fight—to bring their gold and wealth and their pioneer-strong spirit to the side of the North and rally their men to become Union soldiers.

Luke pressed closer to the neck of his agile mare and held on as he ducked under some branches for the horse knew the path he raced better than or as well as Luke did. Her hooves clicked on some smooth stones, pounded into the earth as they galloped on.

What a wonderful world God has given us! Luke thought. He breathed in a deep breath of pine and spring flowers. His horse jumped a sparkling, clear creek and quickly continued along the way. After months of traveling the path, both horse and rider knew the way without much thought.

How could a war be what God wants? Luke contemplated. He had seen the death and destruction that Indian raids had done to both tribe and cavalry; neither were the victor. *How can this be any different than what was about to happen?* Luke had mixed thoughts on carrying the news that would precipitate a war. Bound to his oath and duty, he rode steadily on.

Each day, with each ride, Luke saw the telegraph poles being erected and knew that when they were completed, news could travel West within hours. The Pony Express would no longer be needed to carry the news. Trains and railroad tracks were already in Nebraska Territory, just waiting to push West with goods and people. Luke realized more than ever that the days he had grown up with were soon to be lost in the past. This year of riding for the Pony Express was the most important one of his life, and he would never forget them.

Soon Luke would have to decide if he would fight for his Southern states or hide out in the mountains until the storm of war had passed. *How can I let my Texas family and friends wear a uniform for the Confederacy without me? How can I fight against them?* Luke would be glad when this conflict was over. All of his life it had loomed over him. His grandfather Lucas had preached on it all the days he could remember. As a youth, Luke had thought it would never come, and now he rode with the news beneath him.

Lost in his thoughts, Luke had covered the miles quickly, and his pony stopped abruptly at the next station. News was passed by the station workers as riders went to and fro.

"Today..." Cliff said as he jumped down and held the fresh horse so the next rider could be on his way. "...just got news from the boss that wages will be delayed. The government still hasn't given the contract to us, so we can't be paid, and Mr. Majors, Mr. Russell, and Mr. Waddell are running low on funds. Keeping this going for over a year with no government money to support or pay wages has been tough. They are trying to last, knowing what they do is important in these times. I figure the war or telegraph lines and railroad will shut us down anyway. It's been a good ride for a long while anyway."

Luke knew the government contract to pay wages was important, but he didn't like the "no paycheck that week"—though he had made plenty. "I heard that Butterfield Stage was moving out of Texas since they seceded. Wonder how that will affect the mail?"

"I don't know, but news is happening so fast with changes of all kinds around us. They are calling for soldiers in the South. Are you going to join? Our days are numbered here as it is." He paused and spit out a chaw of tobacco. "Texas voted 166 to 7 to secede. Even old President John Tyler went to Washington to try to help work out a desperate compromise to save the Union. At least that's what the paper said."

Luke was surprised to hear that the mountain man could read.

Cliff continued, "Tyler said the eyes of the whole country are turned to this assembly in expectation and hope."

Luke stood silent, thinking on the news he had just heard. He realized he would need to make a decision sooner than he had originally thought.

"Luke?" his friend and boss asked again.

"Well, I'm not sure yet what my Texas family is thinking on. What about you?"

"Me? Well, I was a fur trapper in these mountains before they convinced me to turn my cabin into a station for this operation. So I think I might just wait it out here. I don't like fighting Indians or a government. Don't make me a coward or anything. I just don't have a stake in it. I'm not gonna fight for a rich Southerner or a black man to be free or stand with an Irish immigrant in Union blue who happens to want a paycheck and doesn't have a clue about why he's fighting."

Luke could tell his friend had been thinking about the matter and was informed on the issues. "Well, I just might tag along with you till the last cannon's fired." The words, once spoken, twisted in his gut and didn't settle well. At that moment, he knew he would have to stand with his family and do what they did.

Chapter 29

"Any updates on the state of our country?" Thomas asked Samuel as he pulled out his chair and sat down at the dinner table. Everyone in the family had gathered at the evening meal. The spring weather was balmy and pleasant, so the little girls were eating on the porch with the door open. Their giggles floated in to where the adults sat to eat.

"We all want the news," Liz said as she looked at Thomas. "But let's pray first. We need His guidance now more than ever before."

"Liz, you're so right," Thomas patted her hand. "Let's pray." The family bowed their heads to give thanks and ask for wisdom for them and the nation.

When the prayer was finished, Liz looked at Samuel. "Okay, now you can tell us what you know, but we aren't going to spend all our time at the table with this talk."

Samuel smiled at Liz. "Yes, ma'am," he responded graciously. "I'm sad to report that Governor Sam Houston has resigned after Texas became the seventh state to submit secession papers to Congress. He was loyal to our great state but also to the Union. The thought of a civil war bothers him greatly. He won't join either side as no good will come from any of this. The Governor said that Edward Clark is now the governor. In fact, he has already moved into the mansion in Austin."

The others ate slowly as they listened. Jackson and Megan, Liz and Thomas, Abby and Emma, along with Tex were all at their supper table that evening. Lydia, just a year old, sat with the grownups. She smiled and babbled as she ate.

"Montgomery, Alabama, is currently the Confederate capital, but talk is it will move to Richmond, Virginia, at any time. Part of Virginia has separated off and is now West Virginia. Four more states have joined the Confederacy, and four slave states have stayed with the Union. Much pressure was applied on them as well. They are divided among their loyalties but Maryland, Delaware, Kentucky, and Missouri voted to stay Union," Samuel stated with a shake of his heard. Texas wasn't the only one that had a hard time with this decision.

Samuel took a bite of the food on his plate as the conversation paused.

"The disbanded Rangers are joining forces again to keep the peace in Texas now that the Union forces are gone, and Robert E. Lee has left to lead the Confederate army," Tex added to what Samuel had shared. He looked at Jackson and said, "Jackson, we will keep you on here in Fort Worth. You can be close to your family, and it will be good to have your experience here in this vital time. You know everyone and are respected. We can trust you. We might have to deal with Northern spies. Liz, keep your eyes and ears open at the Mercantile. They haven't forgotten about the Texas cotton crop for their northern factories. Cotton will now be ferried south on the Rio Grande. Emma, you, too, can receive information in your eating establishment. You two could play a vital role for Texas."

Emma looked at Tex in surprise and listened. *A spy?* Yes, she would be on the lookout and nodded at Tex.

"Of course," Liz nodded. Just thinking about being aware of her surroundings and watchful of any trouble was what she usually did anyway.

"Are the Confederate men signing up yet?" Abby asked.

"Yes and no," Tex said, "we have a list started, and the posters are up. The Texas men were told they would be contacted as needed. Lincoln has asked for a 90-day enlistment of the Union troops. The Southern men started converging so quickly, it scared them some. I'm sure Texas will start any time, although they want Texans to defend Texas and the supplies for the South. This far west, we can hold it securely from the North and continue to grow cotton plus supply cattle for the Confederacy. They need our wealth, cotton and cattle." Tex added, "Watch for rustlers, Thomas."

The reality of war and the part Texas would play was rapidly becoming clearer to them all. For a brief moment in time, the women felt more secure as their men would remain in their state, closer to home.

"The North thinks we are simply farmers and ranchers, friendly and hospitable people. And we are, but we must watch for the wolf among us!"

With those words of caution from Samuel, the conversation turned to crops and cattle. Liz looked at the other women sitting at the table and smiled in relief. No guns and cannons would be rolling into town or men riding away from town, never to return—not yet anyway!

Chapter 30

Summer 1861

The Mailly family had planted an orchard the first spring they had arrived in Texas. Peach and pecan trees were now thriving and providing enough for them to sell at the Mercantile. Emma even had enough to make fresh desserts and specialty dishes in her restaurant. Everyone enjoyed the peach harvest during the long days of summer.

Living in the woods at the edge of the orchard was a confident red fox. Ol' Red would come out of the shadows in broad daylight to make a run on Emma's hen house on a regular basis. Over the past weeks of spring, he had grown even braver and more clever with his daring raids on Emma's chickens. He seemed to feel a chicken dinner was at his convenience any time. The fox was more daring than Luke's wolf pup had ever been.

Emma walked out the restaurant door to check on her nesting hens and the newly hatched Banty chicks. She thought she might as well pick a few peaches while she was at it. Emma hoped that some early peaches would be ripe enough for a cobbler.

But the fox was always on Emma's mind, and just in case, she carried a Colt with six rounds in the revolver's chamber.

A few peaches were ready, and she placed them in her basket. As she turned to walk back, Emma caught a glimpse of the red, furry tail of the fox slip behind the berry bushes. She set down her basket, pulled out her Colt, quietly cocked the hammer, and slowly crept toward the berry thicket. The fox ran out, and she fired twice at him.

He leaped across the openness of the orchard, with Emma following, trying to get a good view of him before she fired any more rounds. She looked in all directions but knew that once again, she had lost the sly animal!

Walking back to where she had left her basket, Emma heard horses and men talking. She grabbed her skirt and lifted the hemline a few inches to run. Walking in the back door, she put her gun and basket on the front work table and quickly went to the front window. A small group of Confederate soldiers wearing smart-looking uniforms had begun dismounting. She noticed that two of them wore decorated coats with gold fringe and gold bars on their cuffs. They looked around and pointed to her restaurant. Boldly, they came up the steps and walked in.

"Good morning, ma'am," one soldier greeted Emma with a smile. "Do you have a meal we can buy? We have been on the road a while and would appreciate a good, home-cooked meal."

"Of course," Emma replied, still taking in the look of the officers. "Have a seat. I have fried chicken, beans, biscuits, and mashed potatoes all in the warmer. If you aren't in a hurry, I'll have fresh peach cobbler in about an hour or so."

"That's certainly more than good enough—a round for all of us. You got that much?"

"Yes, sir!" Emma went to pick up her gun and basket of peaches from the table where the men would sit.

"That's a nice gun you have there," one soldier said as he pulled out his chair to sit. "You know how to use it?"

"Yes, I do—especially on that red fox out back at my hen house or at people who don't like my cooking," she added in a teasing tone. However, the soldiers didn't know Emma and therefore didn't know how to take what she said.

The blonde commented quietly to the officer, "You'd better sweet talk that woman if you want her to cook for you!"

They all enjoyed a hearty laugh. "Where did you get your Colt revolver, ma'am?" the dark-haired man asked as soon as the laughter ended.

He seems to be the boss, Emma thought. "You can buy one next door at the Mercantile if you want. This one was a gift from a Ranger." Emma placed the gun under her counter where she always kept it—just like Liz did next door.

"You hear, boys? She's got a Ranger as a friend who trusts her with a Colt."

"Better mind your manners. If you want any of that peach cobbler, you better sweet talk her some," one the men interjected again.

They laughed again, and Emma smiled at the men. As she walked to her stove to ready their plates, the officer in charge spoke again. "We are looking for a man named 'Tex' or 'Samuel Smith.' Do you happen to know them?"

Emma remembered what she had been told about keeping her eyes and ears open—and to be careful who she trusted. "Why do you want those two?"

"Army business," he replied.

"Are you really Confederates?" she looked them over again.

"Oh, that's fightin' words, ma'am. We don't wear Union blue or have yellowbellies." The man who had asked her about the gun teased back at her but looked her over seriously. He quietly said something to the boss. The boss nodded his head in agreement.

Emma brought two heavy-laden plates with golden, fried chicken, steaming pinto beans, and buttery, mashed potatoes.

"Do you know those men?" he asked again.

"I might could find them for you," Emma spoke cautiously, "after

I get the cobbler in the oven." She wasn't in any hurry to do the bidding of this soldier. After all, he was asking about her friends, and she wouldn't give them up without it being for a good reason.

"I surely can wait for that. Thank you."

Emma finished serving the other two soldiers, stirred up the cobbler and placed it in the oven. Refilling the tea glasses, she said, "I'll be right back. Cobbler's fine. You stay put."

The men snickered about *her* giving them orders.

Emma walked out the front door, visited for a moment with Liz at the walk. Liz looked at the soldiers on the other side of the window glass and nodded to them. Emma stopped to check the soldiers' horses and place a few pats on their noses. She noticed one horse held his leg so no weight was bearing on it. She ran her hand down his leg, and the horse flinched.

The soldiers watched Emma and looked at each other. "She might be the one we are looking for," the quiet soldier noted. The boss nodded and watched Emma cross the street to Samuel's office.

"Samuel, have you noticed the soldiers eating at my place? They are asking for you or Tex."

Samuel looked up quickly. "How did I miss that? I was just reading this telegram. Okay, thank you. I'll be right over."

"Got a cobbler in the oven," Emma added as she nodded and walked out. She looked both ways on the street and let a wagon pass. She walked back up the restaurant steps and in her door.

Within a few minutes, Samuel came into the restaurant. "Good day, gentlemen. I'm Samuel Smith," he extended his hand out to greet the men.

Emma stood close enough to hear the conversation. She appeared to be wiping down the wet flatware she had rinsed with steaming water, but she was actually listening.

The dark-haired man, who Emma had thought was the boss, stood and shook Samuel's hand. "I'm Major-General Crayton. This is Sergeant Spencer and Privates Bueller and Milburn."

Emma noted that the blonde, whose name was Spencer, and the quiet man were privates. Samuel pulled up a chair from another table and sat down with the men. They talked quieter, and she couldn't hear without awkwardly going closer.

"We are here to look over this area and to prepare Texas and the men. We need some good Texas cavalrymen to join the ranks. We have had fourteen skirmishes in June, and our first real battle took place at Bull Run, close to Manassas."

Samuel listened intently and saved his questions for later.

"We had Southern troops stationed at the junction there. The Union troops seem unorganized and untrained; their generals are rattling sabers with each, vying for positions in the Army. The leaders leaving the Union and coming to the Confederacy are leaving some big openings. We now have Robert E. Lee, Jeff Davis, and General Jackson has come our way too. We have some of the best officers any military can have if we can take advantage of the North's lack of readiness. Maybe, hopefully, we can win this in due time."

"Tell me about the battle at Manassas Junction," Samuel stated. His telegram had contained bits and pieces of the story, but he wanted the full account from Major-General Crayton.

"The North was caving to public pressure and launched a full surprise attack. They were winning till late afternoon. Our boys were tired and took serious casualties, but then General Jackson arrived with reinforcements, taking them by surprise and pressing in late in the battle. Those rebel boys yelled and took off like they were coming from the gates of Hell." Crayton smiled as he looked at Samuel. "It became almost funny at this point as an audience from the Union capitol had gathered on the hillside that Sunday afternoon. We could see baby strollers, picnic baskets and umbrellas. Those Yankees starting to retreat got mixed up with the city socialites who were watching the battle. They embarrassed themselves right bad. Our boys scared them to death with that rebel yell and pushing back when they thought the battle had been won."

Samuel smiled and even chuckled a little at the telling of the skirmish. "Wait till you see the newspapers with the report. They are being right hard on the Union troops," Private Bueller stated proudly.

"We have the men ready to fight. We want to end it before winter," Sergeant Spencer added. "The Union is scrambling to save face, moving generals around within the ranks. General Scott pushed General McDowell to fight that day. The two generals' confrontation was so out of hand that President Lincoln removed McDowell and replaced him with General McClellan."

"General *George B*. McClellan?" Samuel asked.

"Yes, you know him?" Crayton asked, surprised.

"Yes, I met him when I was in school back East. Can't say I was too impressed with him. He had just returned from Europe where he had been studying wartime cavalry. He was all excited about a new design of a saddle. I found him to be quite boastful."

Crayton understood what Samuel said, nodded and then continued with his objective. "Colonel Benjamin Terry, a Ranger, is going to head up the 8th Cavalry. We want you to get your best together, Samuel. We want to leave by September."

Samuel looked at each man, taking in what the soldier had said.

Emma had now dished up the hot cobbler into bowls and had placed them on a tray. After walking over, she set it down near the table where the men were talking. She heard the last part of their conversation.

Crayton looked at the steaming dessert and took a whiff of the aroma, settling around the table. Then he said to Samuel, "You know this woman?"

Samuel snickered. "Sure do. I married her sister."

"Does your wife cook like this?" Bueller asked as his spoon dipped down into the golden, floating crust for a second time.

Samuel quickly swallowed a bite of hot cobbler. "No one cooks like Emma!"

"Miss Emma," Crayton replied, "you are a young woman of many talents. I have seen in a short time that you cook, handle a Colt, are cautious of strangers' asking questions, and you know horses. I think the Army has a job for you. We will assign you a code name of 'Peach Cobbler.'" He smiled, but she could tell he was also quite serious. "Miss Emma, brother-in-law Samuel, will you consent to her being a spy for us when duty calls?"

Emma couldn't believe what she had just been asked. She stepped back and looked at each of the men as they stared at her, waiting for an answer. Samuel also looked at Emma as he waited for her answer. She slowly nodded.

Samuel looked at Crayton and asked, "Can we keep her safe? Close to home?"

"We would strive to do so," the Major-General replied.

With the appointment settled, Emma said, "You need to get that horse tended to. I've taught Luther Wheeler how to make a lavender tincture—for lame horses." She nodded at the horse out front and looked at each man with intent in her voice. She was serious with her comment, "I don't know how you feel about a free, black man, but Luther at the livery stable is a good man who does a more than good job. You tell him I sent you and don't give him any trouble." She paused and, as serious as the young Emma could be, added, "You will have to deal with me, and I deal with your stomach!" With those orders issued, she looked squarely at each man. The men listened and then looked to Samuel.

"You better believe her and do as she says," Samuel warned the men. "Luther's just down the street, halfway to Hell Avenue."

"Hell Avenue?" Sergeant Spencer repeated.

"Yes, the gambling halls and saloons are right over the rise." Samuel pointed in which direction. "You might meet up with Sheriff Jackson, also a retired Ranger, and a brother-in-law of sorts."

"So there's more women like Miss Peach Cobbler here?" Crayton asked with a smile.

"The Mailly women from Louisiana," Samuel replied, "blew in here with eight wagons a few years back and pretty much put the town on the map after Major Ripley left with the Army. Liz runs the general store. Her husband Thomas has the best Comanche horses in the state and runs cattle. Her sister Megan is the wife of Sheriff Jackson. Cousin Emma here, you have met, and her sister Abby is the schoolteacher and my wife."

The conversation ended as Mattie rushed through the door with Sofie and Lydia in tow. "Em," she said as she gasped for breath. "Ol' Red is in your hen house!"

Emma ran for her Colt and rushed through the back door of her restaurant. The little girls watched, knowing what Emma would do. Still holding the hands of her little sister and cousin, Mattie turned to Samuel. "Hey, Mister Samuel," Mattie smiled as she greeted him. She was breathing more normally now.

"Good day, Mr. Soldiers," Mattie turned to look at each one, nodding her head. "I'm Mattie, my sister Sofie and cousin baby Lydia. She's our newest one."

"Hello, Mattie," Crayton said with a smile.

With introductions made, Mattie walked out the door, still in tow of her two younger charges.

Crayton looked at Samuel with a big smile. "I see they are training the next generation of Mailly women."

The soldiers laughed, agreeing with Crayton's comment.

"Yes," Samuel chuckled, "not a male child in the lot except Luke, and he rides for the Pony Express, Horseshoe Creek Division."

The men nodded, "About these Comanche horses, where can we see some of them? Our cavalry needs them desperately."

"I'll send word to Thomas. I'm sure he can have some here fairly soon. When do you want the 8th to be ready?" Samuel asked, back to the matter at hand.

"Soon—as soon as possible," Crayton replied.

A shot rang out from behind the restaurant, interrupting the conversation.

"Does Miss Emma cook fox stew?" asked one of the privates.

Chapter 31

Luther Wheeler, the smithy, held the gate open at the livery for Thomas and Chet to lead their string of horses into the corral. The horses were beautiful and strong with shiny coats and good-spirited training.

Thomas led his herd in, then Chet followed Thomas with his string. The horses circled the enclosed arena and whinnied to each other. Luther opened the adjacent corral where a full water trough was waiting.

"Just put in fresh water, knowing you were coming, Mr. Thomas," Luther nodded a greeting at Chet.

Both men took the ropes from the necks of each animal that bound the horses together. Chet had to spend some extra time freeing some ponies that had become entangled as they had trotted in together.

"They sure look good, Mr. Thomas. The soldiers will be happy to see them," Luther stopped for a moment. "What do you think you will get for them?"

"With these already well-trained and most likely going to officers, I'll get two hundred a head, otherwise, one hundred fifty dollars." Thomas patted a handsome bay that nudged his master and nickered as he walked by.

"Great animal, sir," Luther replied to Thomas. They both admired the horses.

They knew that the horse would be the backbone of the Civil

War. Soldiers were trained to give every opportunity to the care of their animals with grass, wheat and oats. Everything depended on the horses' help. Horses were depended on to move supplies and pull ambulance wagons carrying wounded soldiers. Horses carried both generals and messengers. No matter what the horse was put through, the stalwart animals soldiered on in choking dust, struggling through mud, rushing into battle at a full gallop, or silently creeping backward. They served their masters and did what they were called upon to do.

Major-General Crayton walked up to the corral, put his foot on the bottom fence rail, and leaned in to look over Thomas' herd. "Our Confederate cavalry is superior, and their horses are also superior. Our Southern boys have been on horses most of their lives, and they know how to care for them. Our young men have organized themselves into mounted militia even before the war. Texas is the strongest in that regard, and we aim to capitalize on the Texas' expertise. With the South enjoying their horse races as a sport, we have superior stock that is purebred and swift-footed. We have the Tennessee Walker and the American Saddlebred with their great endurance and comfortable ride. Some smaller, more compact Northern Morgans are part of the cavalry because of their incredible endurance."

He paused as he continued to study the horses Thomas and Chet had brought. "With these Comanche horses, our boys are gonna be unstoppable. These Texas boys have been drilling all their lives to ride daringly and charge with sabers. Their sure shooting with a Colt or a shotgun is also excellent."

"I hear you have a son riding for the Pony Express. Any way you can get him home to ride for the 8th Cavalry?" Crayton asked Thomas.

"We haven't had much communication with him since he left,"

Thomas replied. "But truthfully, with all that's happening, I've expected him any day." He paused, thinking for a moment. "His momma isn't gonna be too happy with his being gone all that long a while and then to ride away for the cavalry."

"I'm sure not," Crayton agreed. "Many a mother and wife will experience some agony in the coming days." He looked at Thomas, "We'll do our best to get them all home safely and quickly."

Thomas nodded silently and looked back to the horses.

Chapter 32

Luke knew the time had come to head back to Texas; he could feel it. *When I get back to the bunk station, I'll pick up my pay and ride south. It's time to be with my family again.*

❧ ❧ ❧

Luke was almost back to Texas. He figured he was nearly two days ahead of his past record when he had headed north to ride for the Pony Express.

Texas was huge—almost eight hundred miles to cross in any direction. Luke had never seen the Virginias, Carolinas, Georgia, or Alabama, but he had been told Texas was as big as all of those states combined! Texas was by far the largest of the Confederate states with 266,000 square miles, boasting a population of over 600,000, most of whom lived on the frontier ranches or homesteads.

By now Luke had heard of the excitement created by the South's youth and college students heading off to the frontlines of the Confederate battles. At his last rest spot, he had crossed paths with a young man named Charlie who said he couldn't wait to see a Yankee. He was afraid the war would be over before he could get there. The next morning Charlie had ridden off before the sun had even risen. Luke thought it was best anyway as the man didn't have real clear thinking and couldn't ride very well either. Luke had honed his skills at riding and knowing exactly how hard and long to push Thunder or any other horse, for that matter.

He had found it hard to bid farewell to Cliff and his other friends at the station. Luke would miss these good boys, especially Will and his horse, Ol' Ragged Jim.

"Hey, Luke," Will said that morning after Luke had told him he was leaving, "I'm gonna leave too and go back to bullwhacking for the rebels anyway. The telegraph poles are going to be finished any day, and this job will be over. Best to move on now. I'll see you in the South."

Luke was happy to receive all of his wages paid in gold and patted his pack on his pony. He was carrying some additional weight, but the gold carried a better value than banknotes.

He caught the headline of a newspaper that stated 100,000 Texas cavalrymen, ages 18 to 45, were needed to ride for the Confederate armies. Experienced, wind-whipped, Indian fighters will engage the Union foot soldiers. Luke chuckled when he read in the story that no Texan would walk a yard if he could ride.

Luke didn't have to push Thunder hard on that last day before he hit the edge of the ranch. Thunder knew he was home to the open range; the horse raced where he once ran free, and Luke felt the horse must be able to feel the fresh straw and the whiff of oats in his stall. Both rider and horse raced toward home.

※ ※ ※

Thomas came from the barn after finishing the task of getting things ready for his absence. Lulu and Poncho would keep the minimum going at the ranch with a few horses, a small herd of cattle and the regular barnyard animals. John and Blue had gone on a large freight ride for Liz as she gathered all she could for the Mercantile. When they returned, Thomas would take the remainder of the horses and cattle on a drive to a Confederate holding area for supplies. Chet, John and Blue would help with the drive then meet up with the rest of the Fort Worth men in the 8th Cavalry. Amazingly, the plan Thomas had carefully thought through over and over again, was holding together. A voice roused him from his thoughts.

"Thomas! Hey, Thomas!" Luke yelled out to his dad as soon as he saw him. Thomas looked up, knowing the ranch was fairly empty. He put one boot in front of the other as he jogged to meet his only son.

Chapter 33

The Mercantile was quiet even though the place was full of the community women. The last few days were full of preparation as the men were leaving for the army of the Confederacy the next day.

Liz had a building in her heart that these women needed courage and direction. They didn't know to whom to turn. She felt their fear and unhappiness with what they were facing. Many of the women had kissed their love goodbye for a cause before, but this time was different. The earth was shaking beneath their feet, and they had no place safe to hide their heart.

"Ladies," Liz called out softly because there wasn't much chatter to talk over. "Later today when you meet with your men and gather your families for your last evening meal, I encourage you, I implore you, to be strong. We are frontier women, and we have borne much. But we are about to come face-to-face with a great unknown—an enemy of great force. Enjoy the evening. Eat and laugh with your family and friends. Make lasting memories for you, your children and your husband. As women, we set the character and the atmosphere for our family. Choose not to cause worry for your children and their father. We will not cry or whine or act out in any way that isn't encouraging to our men or our children. We will not complain. The days of asking why are over; we cannot change what has taken place. We must face what is before us.

"We ourselves will be strong soldiers wearing skirts that our men need to see as they themselves march into the unknown. We are healthy and strong in mind and body. When our thoughts go in a direction that is harmful or unproductive, we need to reroute the thoughts to what is good and pure and helpful. We must guard our hearts and not allow our men to see them breaking. We cannot have their thoughts on the worry of hearth and home but on the battles before them."

Fanny Wilton dabbed at her eyes. Anna repositioned baby Aubrey and reached over with her free hand to hold her friend's.

Megan squeezed her lips together with the seriousness of the moment. Patting Lydia and rocking a little, she scanned the somber crowd of women. Most of them were her good friends, but she knew all of these women in some way. Any casualties among the men would affect all of them.

Liz licked her lips and swallowed. "I want you to write a note of love and encouragement to your man—something he can read each day or, at any moment, pull from his shirt pocket for strength and love. Give it to him as he mounts up in the morning. Tell him to tuck it away in his shirt pocket and read it often.

"You can cry alone with God and each other. Bear your heart and soul in this way. We are all feeling the same sad, worried uncertainty. Let each other know your concerns or needs so we can help each other. The best way to alter your feelings or mood is to praise God. Praising our Father helps to build us up and give us the courage we need to stand another day.

"I see our army of men across the way, starting to disperse. Let's pray and enjoy our time. This evening will go by all too quickly."

With a few glances out the front window to confirm that the men were finished with their meeting, all heads bowed for prayer. Liz watched as each woman walked to her husband, took his hand in hers and walked away. Each lady's smile might have been forced but smiling she was.

Liz sat down behind the counter, took a deep breath and dropped her face to her hands in prayer. *God, tell me what to say!* Finally, picking up her pen and paper, she wrote a note to Thomas first.

My dearest Thomas,

> *Keep this letter of love and encouragement close to your heart. At any time, I want you to take it out to read my thoughts over and over again. Please, my love, know that we will be doing our best to be safe and keep the home fires burning for your return. I will hold our memories close until you return to your family.*
>
> *Each day I will tell Mattie and Sofie how much you love them and keep their memories of you alive. I will try my best to write every little thing they do or say in my journal and in my letters to you. Mattie is so busy with her way of saying and doing, it will be hard to write it all, but I will do my best. I will give each a kiss from their papa each day.*
>
> *I will think of our good times while you are away. I will pray for your quick and safe return.*

Always loving you,

Liz

Liz folded the letter and put it in a sturdy envelope. She placed her hands over it, praying and then kissed it. Then Liz wrote another letter to her son Luke. She stopped to wipe a tear trickling down her cheek. "Oh, Luke," she whispered hoarsely, "you've only been home a few days, and now you're off again—a man to fight in a man's war." Pausing again to wipe another unruly tear, she penned her note to her only son.

My dearest Luke,

It was hard to let you ride away to work for the Pony Express, and now I must kiss you goodbye again. My heart leaped when you returned. What a grand surprise to see you on horseback with Thomas! The few days went by way too quickly. I'm so glad all of you will be together as you ride for the 8th. Keep each other safe and in good spirits. We will do the same until all of our loved ones are home again. You have the best riding men with you—experienced men in horsemanship, quick as lightning and loyal to what they believe in.

Keep my note close to your heart. Know that every night and all through each day, my only prayer is for this fight to be over and for the safe return of our family and friends. My only son, now a man, know that I love you, and I'm proud of who you are.

I will keep your sisters laughing until you return to take back that job you all enjoy so.

Praying and loving you,

Your Mother

Finished with her writing, Liz sat back in her chair, holding her breath and the letters to her heart. She sighed deeply. *I won't allow my thoughts to go to a place that isn't known. I must trust my Heavenly Father with their care.*

My sweet Jackson,

First, I must tell you how much Lydia and I will miss you. You are the dearest man I have ever known besides my grandfather Lucas. You are my gentle giant, quick to fight for what is right, making wise decisions, and always looking at the good for all. We will so miss you until your healthy return.

Let it be known that while you are away, we will take every opportunity to pray for your safety and health. We want you to return to your girls happy and well with no reason for concern. We will daily tell our little ones about their handsome papa and the fight for the Confederacy.

We wish Lee and all his troops wisdom and safety. My heart will be partially empty until you fill it all up again.

Loving you every day,

Your dearest wife Megan and daughter Lydia

P.S. Keep this note close to read often for love and encouragement.

Megan closed her eyes and prayed for her Ranger.

❈ ❈ ❈

My Parker,

Aubrey and Hope, Little Dove and I will miss you greatly until you return to us. We hope this will pass with great speed. We know you will do a splendid job at keeping the hope and spirits high of our friends. I will be praying for yours to be the same. We will enforce your prayers for our men and country daily. You are a wonderful man to us and the others. Now with Smithy gone on before us, you are all we have. Please come back to us, Parker. Your girls and I love you.

Your wife,

Anna

      ❀ ❀ ❀

Oh, Samuel, how do I tell you goodbye when we have only started our life together? It saddens me to think of the time I wasted not being married to you. Not that it would make my heart feel any better today as I write you this letter to encourage you and love you from afar. Put this note close to your heart. It's filled with kisses and prayers for your speedy and well return. The picture in my mind is of you on our wedding day. How handsome you are! You are admirable in your services to your city and country. You have spent so much time keeping the people informed so wise decisions can be made for the good of the country. Now at this point, we hope it passes quickly and to the side we bleed for.

My beloved, return to me unharmed and well. Know that your women at home are banding together in prayer and safety each day, waiting for the return of our men. Keep me close to your heart.

Love,

Your wife Abby

Abby concluded her letter by drawing a heart at the bottom of the page and writing the letter "S" on one side and an "A" on the other. Even as she folded the page, she thought her heart would break.

※ ※ ※

Hello Chet,

Now it is my turn to write a letter to you. You must know how much I have enjoyed them and our time together. I keep them in a tin in my kitchen, and I read them often. I'm not sure what gave you the thought to do so, but they do make me smile. It brightens my heart for us to be talking again.

The women here are strong, and we will rely on each other. Please bring all of our family and friends of the 8th Cavalry back to Fort Worth. Concentrate on your duties to finish in due time. The streets and our homes will be quiet with all of you away. We gain strength, knowing you are together and will fight and care for each other. I know you will be missing my food, but I hope you will miss me some too. Take good care of these beautiful horses you all rode away with. They are fighting Confederates too.

Already missing you at my table!

You're in my thoughts and prayers.

Miss <u>Em</u>

Emma read her letter over again, wanting every word to sound exactly right. As she reread the closing of the letter, she underlined "Em." Only Chet and Mattie called her by that term of endearment, and she was pleased.

※ ※ ※

Not much sleeping took place anywhere in Fort Worth that night. In spite of her sleepless night, Liz rose early anyway—not in anticipation for the day, but in perseverance, knowing she would be leading her family and the other women.

The men were leaving, riding out as the 8th Cavalry under the command of Benjamin Terry. Most of the Texas groups had adopted nicknames, and their unit comprised of Rangers, ranchers, and frontiersmen, which would be known as "Terry's Texas Rangers," was already experienced and wise in battle.

Anna and Parker were first to say goodbye. "I love you, Anna. Keep the girls safe." He kissed her, hugged the little ones, and branded their faces in his mind.

Little Dove hugged her adopted father as she said, "You be safe and come back." She handed a small feather to Parker. He accepted her token of love and asked a question with his eyes. "It is a warrior feather," Little Dove explained, "fierce in battle, strong in faith."

"Thank you," he said. "I will keep it on me at all times."

Little Dove nodded, trying not to cry.

Anna handed Hope Rose to Little Dove. She stepped closer to her husband. "Keep this with you too, and read my words often." She stopped, almost choking on her tears she held at bay. Anna kissed him again.

"I love you," Parker said again and then looked at his daughters. "I love you all." He slid the letter into his chest pocket and saddled up, signaling to the others.

Emma called out, "Chet!"

He turned and saw her quickly coming toward him. She carried a cloth bag laden with food, which she placed in his hands.

"Share with the others," she teased, never once avoiding his eyes. He tied a knot over his saddle horn for the treats and smiled. Emma hugged him and pressed the note into his hand. "My turn!" she smiled sweetly.

Chet wanted to hug her again and place a kiss on her sweet lips, but he held back. Their relationship was progressing well, and he didn't want to destroy what he had worked so hard to mend. So he decided to wait. "I'll be home soon…" he paused, "but first, we have to find out if they're yellowbellies under those blue coats!" With a big smile, he swung up on his horse.

In two long strides, Jackson was at Megan's and Lydia's side. He wrapped his arms around them both. "I love you, girls." He pulled back and comforted Megan with his words. "It's just another ride. I'll be back home before you know it."

Megan bit the side of her lip, "I pray so. I love you." Megan watched from the street as he saddled up. "Oh, wait! Wait!" She quickly went to him as he waited astride his horse. "Here, Jackson, put this letter from us where you can read it every day."

Jackson leaned down to take the envelope, nodding his head in understanding and spoke no words. He watched her back away with Lydia in her arms, unaware of the danger ahead.

Abby and Samuel walked out of his office together. He patted his pocket where he had tucked in her letter.

"I know we have already said everything, but I have to say it again." Tears had begun to form in Abby's eyes. She tried to hold them back but couldn't.

Samuel hugged her and kissed her forehead. "Goodbye, my love." He stepped down from the walk and gathered the reins of his horse. Looking around, he noted that all were saddled up except Thomas and Luke. They stood on the porch of the Mercantile with Liz and her two little girls.

"Think of me, my love," Liz said as she handed her letter to

Thomas. She would not allow herself to shed any tears, but her eyes expressed far more than words.

"You know I will." Trying to keep the parting as light as possible, Thomas bent down to his girls, "Be good. I love you."

"Love you too, Papa," Mattie sang out.

Sofie kissed his cheek.

Liz extended her hand to Thomas, and the two walked together to the street. She stood by as Thomas mounted, and then she turned to Luke. "I love you. Be safe. Take care of each other." Luke hugged his mother, kissed her on the cheek, and vaulted into his saddle as only a Pony Express rider could.

She looked down the street to see Ranger Tex and Ranger Colt leading an entourage of riders, including Mr. Wilton, Jeremiah Longmont, Leon DeJarnette, Peter Graham, Nate Turner, and Thayer Tate. These were all the men they had known, respected and loved since they had arrived in Fort Worth. Peter, Nate and Thayer rode over to their friend Luke. The other men filled in wherever there was an opening. Chet, Blue and John were already at the edge of town, waiting with a small herd of cattle and an extra string of horses for the men of the 8th Cavalry.

Slowly, one by one, the women filled the street. Liz reached out to grasp the hand of Abby and Megan as each woman reached for the hand of another. Gradually, they all stood united in body and soul in the dusty street of Fort Worth, watching as the men they loved rode away.

As Chet waited for the men to join them, he watched as Ft. Worth's women, including the one he loved, stood resolute with joined hands, forming one strong thread of courage.